Dear Reader,

Don't you just love shoes? The colors. The styles. The patterns. The most adorable pair of pink, polka-dotted, four-inch— Sorry, I digress. But I do think there's something magical with women and shoes. It's long been a stereotype. But for me, still true. So, along came Lily....

Lily and I shared this common bond of shoe loving, as well as a tendency to be dramatic, so we created shoes for this story together. (The IRS should take special note of my "research" budget for this particular project.) We decided that only one thing was better than having a job as a successful shoe designer....

That was to have a hunky, patient assistant like James Chamberlin at your beck and call. Especially one who understands the delicate balance between income and expenses.

I hope you enjoy James and Lily's story. Visit my Web site at www.wendyetherington.com or write to P. O. Box 3016, Irmo, SC 29063 anytime to get information on new releases.

Happy reading!

Wendy Etherington

"What have I done to you? You're the one who was sitting there looking all cute and irresistible and sexy."

Lily clamped her hand over her mouth. She *hadn't* just admitted that.

James grinned. Then, as if he remembered who she was—and who he was—he shook his head. "I think we've moved into a strange area here."

With her hand still over her mouth in case she said anything *else* embarrassing, she nodded.

He stood up, then walked across the room and toward the office door. "I refuse to let this mess up my agenda. I have plans for my life, a schedule to keep, and you're not on it." He walked through the door, slamming it behind him.

Lily flinched. A marriage proposal from one guy and skid marks on her lips from another. Dating in the twenty-first century was just too damn complicated.

If the Stiletto Fits...

Wendy Etherington

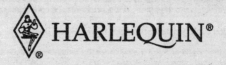

HARLEQUIN®

TORONTO • NEW YORK • LONDON
AMSTERDAM • PARIS • SYDNEY • HAMBURG
STOCKHOLM • ATHENS • TOKYO • MILAN • MADRID
PRAGUE • WARSAW • BUDAPEST • AUCKLAND

ISBN 0-373-44203-3

IF THE STILETTO FITS...

Copyright © 2004 by Wendy Etherington.

This edition published by arrangement with Harlequin Books S.A.

® and TM are trademarks of the publisher. Trademarks indicated with ® are registered in the United States Patent and Trademark Office, the Canadian Trade Marks Office and in other countries.

www.eHarlequin.com

Printed in U.S.A.

ABOUT THE AUTHOR

Wendy Etherington was born and raised in the deep South—and she has the fried chicken recipes to prove it. Though a voracious reader since childhood, she spent much of her professional life in business and computer pursuits. Finally giving in to those creative impulses, she began writing, and in 1999 she sold her first romantic comedy. She's an active member of Romance Writers of America and has been a finalist for the Georgia Romance Writers' prestigious Maggie Award. She writes full-time from her home in South Carolina, where she lives with her husband and two daughters.

Books by Wendy Etherington

To my editor, Jennifer Green,
who guided me through this book
with patience, style and class.

1

LILY REAVES STROLLED through the door of her Manhattan office, still admiring her new shoes. One-of-a-kind Lily's. Would celebrities someday say her name with the same reverence they did Manolo or Prada?

Well, maybe she wasn't in their league *yet*, but she was definitely on her way. Had she, a girl who'd grown up on a farm just outside Des Moines, really made a success of her life in the big city? Sometimes the very idea took her breath away.

She examined her reflection in the gilded, floor-to-ceiling mirror on the reception-area wall. The pale yellow ankle-strap stilettos with pink rhinestone butterfly accents she wore would be one of the standouts of her spring collection.

As she started down the hall that led to the rest of the offices and the workroom where she did her designing, she noted that the chair behind the black marble, semicircle receptionist's desk was empty. A glance at her watch—a "five-dolla" one off a street vendor on Sixth Avenue—proved it was in fact the middle of the day.

She shook her head. Where *was* that girl? Again.

After dropping her purse onto the chair, Lily strode down the wooden-floored hallway toward her assistant/business manager's office. James Chamberlin sat at his always-neat mahogany desk, making notes with his favorite pen as he held the phone between his ear and shoulder. Not a dark brown hair was out of place, and though he'd removed his suit jacket, his navy tie and white dress shirt were in place and pressed to perfection.

"I know, but you'll have to shuffle those. The Spectacular gets top priority."

He paused, listening, and waved her to the chair opposite his desk.

"Did you use the organizational model I gave you last week?" He paused again, raising his eyebrows. "Well, maybe that's the problem."

That controlled, measured, I'm-in-charge-here voice of his sent ripples of tension through the bodies of most people. But then that was a good thing. He was on her side, after all.

And she was lucky to have him. He was the premier assistant on either coast. He'd managed the business interests of Grammy winners, top executives, A-list directors. And now her.

He also loved and respected his mother. How cute was *that?*

In fact, his mother was the reason Lily had had the invaluable James to run her business for the last nine months. She was a big lover of the theater, and James's parents were award-winning stage actors. She'd attended one of their plays and waited outside the stage door afterward like a starstruck fan to get their autographs.

She and the vibrant, free-spirited Fedora Chamberlin had become instant friends. One day over lunch, she'd shared her desperation to find someone to manage her growing business, and, lo and behold, Fedora's only child, James, was the answer. At the time he'd been working in L.A., and his mother had been looking for a way to lure him back to New York.

James had ditched the temperamental director he'd been working for and shown up at her door with his professionalism, sharp mind and patience for her occasional—okay, maybe *frequent*—mood swings and lack of organizational skills. Because of him, Lily Reaves Shoes had become a sensation. Because of him, she'd landed the Spring Spectacular. In just a few weeks, three of the hottest clothing designers in the city were being featured in a star-studded fashion show. And each and every model would be wearing shoes she'd designed.

"Fine. Just get back to me later today." He hung up the phone and glanced at her. "So, how did it go?"

She stood, propping her foot on the chair so he could see the stilettos. "Great, huh?"

"Look damn uncomfortable to me."

"I'm not asking you to wear them."

She cast a sideways glance at him, mildly annoyed he hadn't even complimented her trim bolero jacket and slim skirt with matching butterfly appliqués. One of the Spectacular designers had sent the outfit to her after she'd sent several large-size shoes to his sister. In a city overflowing with overpriced clothes, a girl had to find bargains where she could.

Of course, James zeroed in on the bottom line. Not her hair, which she fought with on a daily basis. Or her clothes, or her legs, which the production manager had seemed most impressed by.

He studied them a moment, his gray eyes narrowed in concentration. "The craftsmanship is excellent. I like the sheen of the leather. The design is decent."

Gushy was not the word to describe James. But then, she paid him for organization and managerial direction, not compliments. Lily plopped back in the chair, smoothing her skirt and crossing her legs. "Where's Garnet?"

"Lunch."

"For how long?"

He glanced at the antique brass clock on the wall. "Too long. As usual."

"Did you check her feet?"

"Yes."

"If I catch her wearing just one more pair…"

James sighed, looking completely unconvinced by her warning tone. "I know, you're going to fire her."

"Why did I hire her again?"

"Because one of your most important clients asked you to."

"He *begged*, remember?" Recalling yesterday, when her sneaky receptionist had sneaked to a club with a pair of pumps Lily had designed for a special display window in Bloomingdale's, she sighed. "And I'm beginning to understand why."

"You won't fire her, Lily."

"Sure I will."

"Prove it."

Smiling, she leaned forward. "I do believe you're trying to goad me, James Chamberlin."

He lifted his hands, palms out. "Would I do that?"

"Sometimes I think you'd do just about anything to see Garnet sail out that door for the last time."

"With *your* shoes on her feet, don't forget."

Leaning on his desk, she propped her hands underneath her chin. Garnet had potential; she just needed direction. And focus. And ambition. Lily had had all those things when she'd first come to the city and she still struggled with her confidence sometimes. "Her father helped me out at a time when I really needed orders."

"I know. I was only kidding." He paused. "Sorta."

"Garnet just needs some direction. Weren't you ever young and aimless?"

"No."

Studying his perfectly serious face, she could imagine that was true. James not only always knew where he was going, he knew three different ways to get there and had the entire trip clocked in hours, days, weeks, miles to go and expected weather forecast.

Lily had glanced at his daily agenda once and had immediately been nightmarishly transported back to eighth-grade social studies when she was expected to write essays with mind-boggling Roman numbers, bibliographies, indexes, even footnotes. And everything indented and lined up to perfection. The thought still gave her the chills.

"Can you at least talk to her again about my phone messages?" he asked. "She has no system. Some she writes down—on pink pads that she's also doodled little hearts all over. Some she e-mails me—though she usually transposes or leaves off numbers. Some she actually manages to send to voice mail—though usually to your mailbox instead of mine."

"I'll talk to her," she promised. Though most of the inner workings of computers mystified her—and, frankly, sometimes intimidated her—e-mailing was like socializing. *That* was a concept she understood. "Did you get the contracts for the Spectacular yet?"

James held up the stack of papers in front of him. "Right here."

Lily pressed her lips together, hesitating to ask the question that had plagued her since she'd been offered the job. "And my name's really on them?"

He pushed the contracts toward her. "Of course it is."

Though she clearly saw her name at the top, her eyes crossed at all the wherefortos, therefores and such. "Does everything look okay?"

"There are some phrases I'm asking them to alter, but other than that, everything is in order."

Looking up, she met his gaze. "Have I told you lately how much I appreciate you?"

"Lily, you earned this. They came to us, remember?"

She shook her head. She'd been floundering in mediocre-ville before he'd arrived. Her only break had been two years ago, when an Oscar-nominated actress had broken the heel of her shoe just before walking down the red carpet and had grabbed the ones her assistant wore—a pair Lily had designed. An industry buzz had ensued, but one she hadn't capitalized on until James arrived.

This year, he'd contacted the right people in L.A. and arranged for her to work with several Hollywood stylists to design dozens of shoes for entertainers attending the awards shows. Lily could hardly wait for the broadcasts to see which ones made the cut.

"I wouldn't be here without you," she said.

His lips tipped up on one side. "Well, I *am* the best…"

At the sight of his half smile, she blinked. James was so serious most of the time that it wasn't until he actually brightened up that she realized how handsome he was. Not that he wasn't attractive when he wasn't smiling. He was. In a buttoned-up, conservative way.

Not her type, but then that was a good thing, since he'd made it very clear from the moment he'd come to work for her that their relationship was strictly business. Fine by her. She needed an assistant to keep her on schedule, to manage her contracts and business affairs, to work with her accountant on managing her money. Lovers she could find on her own.

Though mediocre-ville could probably also describe that area of her life at the moment. She either managed to find guys who wanted a passive, stay-at-home wife and a dozen kids, or one-night-stand louses.

"But only because of my long experience," James finished. "You don't need me as much as you think."

"Oh, yes, I do."

He gave her an odd look.

Before she could question him, though, a familiar voice echoed down the hall. "Hellooo…"

"She's back."

James's eyes actually pleaded. "The messages?"

Lily rose and headed toward the door, enjoying the feel of the four-inch heels on her feet. Maybe she'd wear them on her date tonight. She did enjoy seeing a man goggle. "I'm going, I'm going."

"I need to talk to you before you go out tonight."

She stopped in the doorway. "What makes you

think I'm going out? I could be staying in with a book and a soothing cup of tea."

"Right. Even *I'm* going out tonight."

"Out? Like a date?"

Raising his eyebrows, he leaned back in his chair. "I do have them occasionally."

Lily recalled a brunette he'd brought to a cocktail party not long ago. The woman had been quiet and sweet—just the kind of date she'd expect James to choose. What *was* her name? Kate? Karly? Kelly. "Where are you and Kelly going?"

"I'm not going out with Kelly anymore. This is someone new."

"Oh." She waved. "Well, have fun."

She headed down the hall and reached Garnet just as she was rounding the receptionist station.

"Look at the *adorable* bag I bought today."

Despite her frustration, Lily had to smile. Garnet did have a great sense of fashion.

The bag looked just like a Chinese take-out carton, even down to the silver wire as a handle, except that the carton was covered in red-and-black satin. She took the bag, rubbing her fingers across the fabric. "It's really great, Garnet, where—" She broke off as she recognized the small tag sewn on the bottom. "This is a Fabian LaRoche."

Garnet took the bag back and danced around in a circle. "I know. Isn't it the cutest!"

"This is a five-hundred-dollar bag. You don't make that in a week."

Garnet waved her hand and set the purse on her desk, admiring it like some people would a priceless artifact. "I put it on my AmEx. Daddy gets that bill."

Lily opened her mouth automatically to advise her employee that she should take some responsibility for her own finances, but then remembered Garnet didn't work for money. This was just her way of placating her father until she turned twenty-five and could get full control of her trust fund.

Raised in a strictly middle-class household, Lily wanted to pooh-pooh the excess. But this was the world she now lived in. She smiled. Ah, the sacrifices of living in the Big Apple.

Deciding a change of subject was in order, Lily leaned against Garnet's desk. "We need to talk about phone messages."

Garnet rolled her eyes. "Again?"

"James is having trouble getting accurate ones."

"It's not my fault! It's that computer." Garnet pointed to the screen beside her on the desk. Lowering her voice, she added, "It makes weird noises sometimes, and then I get this yellow exclamation-point thing and an error message." She shuddered.

Lily shared her shudder. She'd seen that message. She glanced at the screen, which currently had a cartoon graphic of a pair of red stiletto pumps dancing across it—a creation by her friend and computer consultant, Gwen. And though she and Gwen could bond most any night over a favorite chardonnay, martini, movie or slice of gossip, she most certainly did *not* share her interest in technology.

"Hmm," she said, trying to seem competent instead of intimidated. "That doesn't sound good. I think James would prefer his messages e-mailed to him, or the caller transferred to his voice mail, if they're agreeable. He's not thrilled with pink message slips with little hearts drawn all over them."

Garnet folded a piece of gum into her mouth. "He could stand to lighten up, you know."

"I know. But he runs the office."

"But you're the boss, right? I mean, I like James and all." She smacked her gum. "But women should stick together, don't you think? I mean, you should understand that—you're a total feminist, so— Hey, cool shoes!" She bent low so she could get a better look at the yellow stilettos. "Wow, these are great! What are you calling them?"

"Misty."

"Tight. When do they hit the stores?"

"Any day now—along with the rest of the spring collection. This is the very first pair out of production."

Garnet leaned back in her chair. "You always do that, right? Take the first pair, I mean. I think that's awesome. See, that's what I mean. A man would never think to make sure each and every one of his shoes was in his personal collection. I mean, really, why are *men* designing shoes for women, anyway?"

This was what talking to Garnet always did to a person. Lily was usually so dizzy after their conversations she generally forgot what she'd started out discussing. She wasn't sure if Garnet's brain was more advanced, or if she was just incapable of holding on to one subject for more than forty-five seconds.

"I really like your philosophy," Garnet continued, mentally zigzagging. "Date a lot, settle on no one."

Lily was mildly uncomfortable being a role model for a twenty-one-year-old. While she and Garnet were only seven years apart agewise, it seemed decades separated them in every other sense. Garnet and the girls she hung out with seemed so jaded and...well, fast—to use an old-fashioned word. She worried about them jumping into life and relationships before they were ready. "I do date a lot, I guess. But you understand I don't sleep with every man I date."

Garnet waved her hand. "Oh, yeah. Lots of scumbags out there who are only interested in getting laid. But how do you feel about blow jobs?"

Lily swallowed. "I, uh—" Wasn't this a conversation a girl had with her mother? Since Lily knew she wasn't ready for kids—and wasn't sure she'd ever be—she certainly wasn't the right person for this.

Quit being goofy. She talked about all aspects of sex with her girlfriends all the time.

Garnet's bright, curious blue gaze was fixed on her face.

"I think you should consider all sexual acts carefully."

Garnet pursed her lips. "That's a good philosophy. Now, about the messages... I promise to e-mail them if he'll take a look at this computer and those weird exclamation points."

Her head still spinning from the tangents they'd veered off on, Lily glared down at her receptionist. "If that was the problem, why didn't you just tell him that?"

Garnet glanced from side to side, then leaned forward and whispered, "Don't tell anybody, but he kind of intimidates me sometimes."

Lily could definitely relate. She and Garnet were talkers. James was most certainly not. She figured Garnet felt the same way she did—quiet people made her nervous. Dead silence was a space she was obligated to fill. "Okay, well, let's see what we can do."

"*You're* going to help with the computer?"

"Hey, I did all this stuff on my own before you two got here." Admittedly not too well, but she'd managed. She leaned toward the phone. "Let's start with the voice mail. I'm extension one, James is extension two. When you need to forward a call to his voice mail you press this button, then this one." Lily demonstrated with a pointing finger.

"And when I need to forward a call to you?"

She'd actually told most anyone she could think of to·call her cell when they needed to get in touch with her. "Same thing, just press this—" She stopped and considered the phone pad and its myriad similar-looking buttons. "How about color-coded labels? Blue for James, pink for me."

Garnet grabbed her arm. "Oh, that's perfect."

They spent a few minutes finding labels, cutting them into two small sections, then coloring them with Lily's sketching pencils. Now that the buttons on the phone were colors instead of numbers, she could only pray Garnet would get things right. She couldn't afford to piss off James and lose his host of office skills.

"Now for the e-mail." Lily eyed the computer with innate distrust, then closed her eyes and pressed the spacebar. When she opened them, the dancing shoes had disappeared, and the main screen was in view. She double-clicked the e-mail program—and who, exactly, had come up with *that* redundant system?— then waited while the computer did whatever it did to accept mail.

A yellow caution sign with an exclamation point

popped up in the middle of the screen. Lily stepped back. "Yikes."

"Told ya."

Lily linked her fingers behind her back. "Let's just—" She scooted away from the computer. "Let's just not touch this anymore. I'll, uh…go tell James."

"Better you than me."

As Lily slinked away from Garnet's station, she noted the receptionist had found an emery board and was filing her nails—hard at work as usual. Lily poked her head around the door frame to James's office, told him about the problem, then darted to her workroom. She had designs to go over.

She spent the next several hours evaluating the sketches she'd made for the Spectacular. One designer wanted her signature color to be bright orange—a hue Lily could relate to—so she'd come up with orange dots, stripes and checks; orange patent leather, bows and wraparound straps; and, finally, orange logos of the designer's crest.

After approving the sketches with her signature, she stretched her arms over her head. She had a lukewarm date to prepare for. Maybe she should get to it. She liked cute designer Brian Thurmond, but she considered them more friendly colleagues than about-to-connect lovers. She'd befriended him a couple of weeks ago at a fashion show, since she understood what it was like to want so badly to succeed, but still be floundering. And connections were gold in the fashion business.

She couldn't find a ton of enthusiasm for the night out, though. He'd spent most of their last date trying—a little too obviously—to convince her to get him into the Spectacular.

She was on her way out the workroom door when Garnet called down the hall, "Li——ly!"

"I'm right here," she said as she ground to a halt in the foyer. "We have an intercom, you know."

Garnet smiled over her shoulder. "Oh. Forgot. Line one. It's your sister."

Suppressing a groan, Lily picked up the extension on the foyer table. "Hi, sis, you just caught me on my way out." Well, she *was* going out—in about two hours, after she showered, redid her makeup, dressed and snacked.

"Out with who?" her older, bossier and nosier sister asked.

"A guy." She knew her sister would never settle for that, so she added, "A fellow designer."

"Do things look—" She broke off as something crashed in the background. "Jack Jr., get out of those cabinets!"

"Maybe you should check on him. I could let you go…"

"No, he's fine. I was going to ask if things look promising between you and this guy."

"I'm not going to marry him, if that's what you mean." Giving up the single life in the city wasn't going to happen anytime soon—if ever.

"Lily, you really need to get busy. You're twenty-eight, you know. When I was twenty-eight—"

"I know. You'd been married for eight years and had two kids already. I'm not you, Karen," she added quietly.

She sighed. "Sorry. I'm nagging again. That's my job."

Lily smiled, relieved her sister wasn't going to

push. Neither of them were very good at understanding the other, but they were family, and that meant something that time, distance and differences in lifestyles could never erase. "And you do it well."

"Thanks for the shoes, by the way. Though I pretended I didn't know when Mom asked how much you charge customers for the ones you sent her."

"Wise move."

"And what was with that extra pair you sent me? The shiny black ones? The heels are way too high. Where in the world would I wear something like that?"

Her sister had great legs, but Lily wasn't sure anyone but Karen had seen them in the last ten years. And Lily couldn't think of anything more depressing than to not have anyplace to wear a great pair of new shoes. "To dinner with your husband."

"In Redwood? Get real."

"Then wear them for Jack around the house."

"With what? Jeans and a sweatshirt?"

"Nothing." She giggled. "I bet I get a thank-you card from Jack."

She spoke with her nieces and nephews—two of each—and promised to plan a trip to Iowa to see them as soon as the Spectacular was over. Even though she wouldn't have her sister's life, she did enjoy visiting her nieces and nephews. Even when she didn't fix her hair, makeup or wear designer clothes and shoes, they just adored her because she'd play Chutes and Ladders for hours on end.

As she hung up the phone, Lily said to Garnet, "I'm gone for the day if anybody asks."

Garnet smacked her gum as she played solitaire on the computer. "Okay. Have fun."

She walked down the hall, then through the door into her private apartment. She had a beautiful space on the twentieth floor that she'd separated into two areas for her offices and apartment. The building had a great uptown address, plus amenities like a small gym, concierge desk and uniformed doorman. Even James had been impressed with the space and had rented an apartment in the same building on the sixteenth floor.

As Lily walked into the den, she passed by the plush seating group covered in plum-and-gold fabric and headed toward the floor-to-ceiling windows that dominated one wall. The sun was just setting, and Manhattan lights were flicking on like fireflies. Soon the suits and briefcases would be replaced by glamorous gowns and bags. The shoppers would become diners. The nightclubs and bars would spring to life, keeping time with the endless pulse of the city.

Just as it had earlier, happiness moved through her. She really had a remarkable life. She didn't have a two-hour commute from the outskirts of the city anymore. She didn't even have to get dressed if she found inspiration in the middle of the night. She had great friends, a challenging career and she'd achieved a level of both creative and financial success that most people would envy.

So, if—every once in a while—she felt as if her life was missing something, she managed to find a project, a new friend, a shopping trip or a party to fill it.

She'd dreamed of this life ever since she was five, and her grandmother had taken them all on a trip to the city. They'd seen a Broadway play, done the tours of the Statue of Liberty, the Empire State Building and all the rest. It had been the most magical five days of Lily's life. She'd come home with a snow globe and the statue inside. She'd gone to bed every night staring at it and wishing for the day she'd finally become a New Yorker.

Waving off the small, lingering slice of emptiness, Lily strode into her bedroom, which she'd decorated in calming creams and golds. Her favorite piece in the apartment was her cherry, four-poster bed. A decorator had helped her pick out a plush duvet and lots of pillows in various sizes and shapes, then hung white fabric along the railings between posts, so she could literally close out the world if she wanted.

For the next hour, she primped—one of her favorite things when she had the time. She was such a makeup junkie, she usually tried out several different looks before settling on one. Then she perused her giant, walk-in closet—complete with custom-made, revolving shoe rack. She needed something semi-sexy but not too obvious.

Since Brian was probably more interested in her industry connections than her legs, she ought to dress accordingly.

She finally decided on a trim black pantsuit with a silver satin camisole peeking between the folds of the jacket. She picked out silver, ankle-wrap, heeled sandals that might hurt like hell if they went dancing later, but they'd look festive.

After she piled her shoulder-length dark hair on top of her head in a loose twist, she strolled back through the den and into the kitchen. She had to eat something so she wouldn't pig out during dinner.

Knock, knock.

Lily paused with her hand on the Parmesan cheese, which she was currently shaking over her slices of reheated pizza. "Yes?"

"It's James."

Well, damn. She'd forgotten all about him. He'd wanted to talk to her before she left.

She shoved a bite of pizza in her mouth, then muttered around it, "Be right there." Opening the door, she found him with his suit jacket now on and buttoned, and a serious expression planted on his face. Well, James was serious most of the time, but this was a new level—even for him. "Come on in."

Hesitating, he glanced past her. "You're alone?"

"Yeah. I'm just getting ready to go out. Sorry I forgot to come by your office."

He still hesitated. He'd been in her apartment many times, of course, but he always seemed slightly out of place. The intimacy probably offended his professional sensibilities.

Lily grabbed his hand and tugged him inside. "Oh, come on. I was just about to pour some wine." She headed to the kitchen, leaving him to trail behind. "Did you ever find out what was wrong with Garnet's computer?"

"The CAT5 cable connection was loose between the router and the modem. I fixed it."

She blinked. She understood about three words in that sentence—and they were *and*, *the* and *it*. "O-kay." As she poured chardonnay into a glass, she asked, "You want some?"

James pulled one of the iron bar stools away from the black-tiled counter and slid onto it. "Sure."

Mildly surprised—he no doubt considered this a

business conversation, not a social occasion—she handed him the glass, then selected another one for herself.

"What's up?" she asked after her first sip. "There's not a problem with the Spectacular, is there?"

He took a healthy sip of wine. "No."

Again, with the serious tone. Curious, but not alarmed—James could get uptight on occasion—Lily snacked on her pizza. "Hungry?"

He leaned forward, peering at the slices. "*Pizza?*"

She grinned. "It pairs well with the chardonnay."

After another sip of wine, he folded his hands on the counter. "I'm not really sure how to say this, so I guess I'll just blurt it out."

Her stomach tightened. Something was wrong. Had orders drastically fallen off? Maybe Bloomingdale's and Neiman Marcus had both pulled their business. "Okay."

He met her gaze. "I'm retiring."

She angled her head. "From what?"

"My job. *This* job. I'm going to finish the last three months of our contract, then I'm—"

"You're *quitting*."

2

LILY'S HEAD actually spun. She gripped the counter for support. He couldn't—he wouldn't—

"I know this comes as a shock," he said gently. "I'd really planned to retire last year, about the time you came along with your offer. But your business seemed like such a challenge, and I just couldn't resist."

Her mama had always said she should have had "Born to be a Diva" tattooed on her butt the moment she was born. And she could feel a massive fit coming on hard. He couldn't do this to her. He was deserting. "*Old* people retire! You're, you're—"

"Thirty-two. But I'm financially set, and I'm ready to get out of the city, out of the rush and craze. I'm ready to settle down. I'm going to Connecticut and open a café."

"Connecticut!" She paced across the tiled kitchen floor. "What's so freakin' great about Connecticut?"

"It's quiet and relaxing. I've already bought the farm. You should see it."

Lily ground to a halt. This was a nightmare. "You bought a *farm?* Like with cows and chickens and stuff?"

He smiled and looked thoughtful. "No animals yet, but there are stables, so I guess I'll get some horses. Or maybe I'll breed dogs. Cocker spaniels or Labradors."

She tried to picture James, suit-and-tie-at-every-hour-of-the-day-and-night James, rolling around a stable with a litter of baby cocker spaniels. Nope. The picture just wouldn't focus.

She'd spent more than half her life on a farm. Her father had grown corn, which he'd sold to make ethanol, and her mother had believed in growing or raising nearly everything they consumed.

The work was backbreaking, hard and mostly thankless. Tractors were expensive and hard to maintain. You were always at the mercy of the weather. Chickens stank. Cows had to be led around by the nose, or they'd get struck by lightning during thunderstorms.

Suave, urban James had absolutely no idea what he was getting into.

Lily wanted to panic. Or scream. She was hitting her creative peak thanks to him. She never had to worry about the business details, because she knew he'd take care of them. He was critical to her business, to her *life*. She absolutely couldn't run either of them without him.

"James, you can't do this. I need you."

"You'll be fine. You were fine before I arrived."

She shook her head, rushing toward him, tempted to jump across the bar and into his lap and bodily force him to stay. "I wasn't fine. I was a mess. I went through two assistants in four months before you came. Before that, I was alone and clueless."

"I'll help you find someone else. Someone who's reliable and understands you."

Knowing she was acting like an idiot but not caring, she poked out her bottom lip. "I want you."

His eyes softened. "You don't need me, though."

"Yes, I—"

"I have to go, Lily." James stood, shoving his hand through his hair as he turned away, walking across the room toward the windows. "I had plans for my life. Plans that didn't include managing spoiled movie stars and out-of-control divas." He glanced at her over his shoulder. "No offense."

She nearly crushed the stem of her wineglass. "Oh, gee, thanks."

He turned back to the view. Darkness had fully enveloped the sky, so the buildings were just a shadowy outline dotted with millions of lights. She knew without standing beside him what he saw when he looked down—the cabs and limos crawling through the streets, the rectangular grid of office buildings set against the silhouette of high-rises, throngs of pedestrians moving like a single determined wave across intersections.

"I'd always planned to go to culinary school," he said quietly. "Or business school. Instead, I wound up managing my parents' crazy career, then their friends', then I became successful and settled on just one client at a time. I was paid well. I enjoyed the change of balancing such a complicated mix of business interests. Even life in jaded, beautiful L.A. was fun once.

"But I want out of the race. I want something else. I want to pick up my life where it veered off course fifteen years ago."

She understood probably better than anybody

how the need to fulfill your dreams was a vital part of life. But she was desperate to hold on to her own dream, and she needed James to do it. He couldn't possibly have thought this through. He didn't realize what he was leaving.

Shoving her wine aside, she stalked toward him. "Why a café? Hell, Starbucks is the wildest place in town."

"My café will be more like a gathering place for the locals. You can read the paper. Exchange news and gossip. Maybe I'll invite book clubs to meet in the evenings. I could learn to make bread and show off my famous cheesecake recipe."

Lily darted around him and planted her hands on her hips. "You can make *cheesecake?*" she accused in a dangerous whisper. She was holding on to her temper by a thread. Fear was desperately trying to push its way through her body. And, at the core of it all, she just plain didn't understand why. *Why* did he want to leave? *How* could he?

He glanced down at her, his eyes bright with affection. "I'll make you the chocolate-turtle one before I go."

The resolved expression on his face made her throat start to close, and not even the promise of cheesecake could cheer her. Her mind darted about for another logical argument. That was the way to get to him. She didn't think he'd respond to tears or terror. "Why Connecticut?" she managed to ask in a strained voice. "You could open a café in the city. We could hire an assistant for you here. You could stay in charge but have more help."

"The commotion of the city is what I'm trying to

escape." He lifted his hand as if he might stroke her cheek, then let his arm fall back by his side. "It's not you, Lily, I promise."

Her hands shook, but she grabbed his arm, turning him toward the windows. Tapping the glass, she asked, "Can you really leave that view, that *energy,* behind? God, James, I want to shake you. The city is the most amazing place on earth. When you have perfection, how could you possibly ask for more?"

"You grew up with trees and wide-open spaces. Stars you can see clearly at night. No subway or pollution in sight. How could you possibly ask for more?"

"I grew up in the boondocks! Have you ever tried to get a decent cappuccino on a farm?"

"I'll make my own."

"What about restaurants and takeout?"

"I'll have those culinary-school classes to fall back on."

"What about shoes?"

"I'd ask you to send them to me, but I really don't think a pair of four-inch stilettos would suit me."

Lily rubbed her temples. She certainly couldn't outwit him, or outthink him. She had to figure out something else. And quick.

"You should get to your date." He glanced at his watch. "Me, too. We'll talk in the morning." He started toward the door.

"What about watches?" she asked as she stalked after him. His calmness made her want to scream in contrast. "I bet they don't sell cool watches on street corners in Connecticut."

At the door, he turned back. "Maybe you'll give me one—as a parting gift." He reached out and grasped her hand, giving it a quick squeeze. "You look lovely tonight, by the way. That silver blouse really suits you. And, of course, it's sparkly—perfect for the luminous Lily Reaves."

He was out the door before she could respond.

And a good thing, too, since she wasn't quite sure she could have resisted slugging him.

Sweet compliments as he destroyed her world by quitting? James Chamberlin had no idea how dirty she'd fight if she was pushed far enough.

No idea at all.

LIGHT-HEADED FROM her third glass of chardonnay and still depressed and frantic over James's announcement, Lily sipped her wine and tried hard to focus on the elegant Manhattan restaurant where Brian had brought her. Black linen tablecloths, roses on the table, fine china and crystal, well-dressed patrons and spectacular service.

He certainly had excellent taste, though part of her worried about the expense. Brian's business wasn't nearly as successful and stable as hers.

"How are the preparations for the Spring Spectacular coming?" he asked.

Lily chewed a bite of salmon slowly to give herself time to prepare an answer to his question. She settled on a simple "Fine."

What if this was the last big show she did? What if James's L.A. contacts dumped her after he left? She *really* wanted to see a pair of her sparkly shoes on that red carpet again. What if—

She cut herself off in an effort to make coherent conversation. "How do your spring orders look?"

Brian shrugged. "Not sure. My business manager handles all that stuff."

Though that was true for Lily as well, she certainly knew on a weekly basis how business was progressing.

"So the Spectacular preparations are going well?"

She sighed. "Yes. As usual, James has everything under control. We're actually ahead of schedule."

"But are *you* okay? You seem distracted."

Lily laid her hand across her stomach. She was regretting this date more by the second. She should have called her friends and spent the night crying on their shoulders. "I think I'm just stressed. It's been an…interesting day."

"Oh." Brian cleared his throat. "Sorry. We've had some great times together, don't you think?"

Struggling to adjust to the change in conversation, she nodded slowly. "Well, yeah, I guess."

He kicked his smile up a notch. "I think we should take our relationship to the next level."

Lily suppressed a wince. "Well, I—"

"Will you marry me?"

Her jaw dropped. "Excuse me?"

"I think we should get married."

This night was just too weird to comprehend. "You're kidding." She waved her hand as he opened his mouth to speak. "Doesn't matter if you're kidding or not. No."

Cute, blond, but obviously hard-of-hearing Brian frowned. "No?"

"We've only been out a few times. Don't you think it's a bit soon to get married?"

He reached across the table and grasped her hand. His blue eyes softened. "When it's right, why wait?"

Lily tapped her nails against the table. *Do you want the whole list, or just the top twenty-five?* "I'm not getting married, Brian."

"We'll have a long engagement."

"Ever," she finished.

"Of course you are, darling. You're lovely and talented, and you need a partner who'll support and understand you."

"That's what a manager is for." With James running her life and business affairs, what did she need a husband for? She wouldn't even think about the possibility that he'd really leave. She would find a way to talk him out of this crazy retirement thing.

Since this was the second time tonight she'd found herself dealing with a man who was dead set on pursing a really bad idea, she figured she'd give the logical argument another swing. "We don't know each other well enough to get married."

"I know you."

"What's my favorite color?"

"Uh…"

"What's my favorite thing to do?"

"Uh…" He broadened his smile. "We'll learn all that."

"Sure we will. It's called dating." There was something very odd about all this—not just odd because she hadn't seen this coming, but suspicious odd. "Don't most men want sex instead of marriage? Or at least sex first?"

His eyes twinkled. "So glad you brought that up… I'm free after dinner."

I'll bet. Sex aside, this was just weird. She and Brian had mild chemistry and business interests in common, but nothing that warranted a proposal. What was really going on? She might be a former farm girl, but she'd lived in the city for ten years. She hadn't just fallen off the turnip truck.

Lily pulled her hand from his grasp, then leaned back and crossed her arms over her chest. "Okay. What's the real deal?"

"We should merge our fashion empires. Think of the possibilities."

"Our—" She didn't have a fashion empire— though that was a promising goal—and she knew *he* didn't have anything *close* to an empire. If he didn't know what his sales were for the spring, he might not even have a business anymore. "So, this is a business proposition, not a proposal."

"I figured a proposal would better appeal to you as a woman."

"A lie, as opposed to the truth, you mean."

He shrugged. "A woman as successful as you needs someone to support her, someone to escort her to functions, someone who won't be offended when she puts her work first."

She gasped. The constant reminders about the Spectacular, the seeming lack of direction regarding his business, the way he'd conveniently forgotten his wallet on their last date. It all suddenly made sense. "You're looking for a sugar mama."

He looked shocked for a second, then laughed. "I thought that had gone out decades ago. It's such a charming expression." Then he stopped abruptly and leaned forward. "Actually, yes, that's exactly what I had in mind."

"I see," she said. She supposed there was still

enough of the farm girl in her to actually be shocked by this jaded idea.

"You need a man who's tied to you legally," he went on. "One you can trust."

"I trust James. You, however, I don't." She rose and tossed her napkin on her plate. "Goodbye, Brian."

Eyes wide, Brian stood as well. "Lily, I'm only trying to help. As a woman, you're in a vulnerable position."

She stalked two steps forward, planted her four-inch stiletto sandals dangerously close to his instep and glared. "Do I look vulnerable to you?"

"Uh, well… actually—"

"Goodbye, Brian." She spun away, almost plowing into the waiter who'd obviously rushed over to see what the problem was.

"Madam, can I get you some more wine?" the waiter asked, his expression carefully bland.

I need a lot more wine, pal. She gave him a wan smile. "No, thank you. I'm leaving."

Brian grabbed her arm. "Do you think you can spot me some cash? I'm kind of tapped out."

How the hell did she get herself into these situations? She glanced at the waiter, who'd stepped back several feet. She crooked her finger at him, and when he stood in front of her, Lily said quietly, "We're going to be splitting the check." She fumbled in her bag for some cash, quickly tallied her dinner, plus a tip to cover the whole check—since she doubted Brian would part with his portion—then slid the bills into the waiter's hand.

She cut her gaze toward Brian. "*He's* on his own." Whirling, she strode out of the dining room without a backward glance. Red-faced with anger and embarrassment, she retrieved her coat, then stepped outside and asked the valet to hail her a cab. After giving the cabbie her address, she fumed in the back seat.

What was with men these days?

The guy she'd dated before Brian had only been interested in a one-night stand. Then she'd met Brian and had found his easy smile and awareness of her industry refreshing. She'd only had a moment of pause over his slightly superior attitude, though most designers had something of an ego, or at least blind ambitions. If you didn't believe in your designs, no one else would. But had she foreseen him being a smiling hyena, looking for a woman to feed off for contacts and financial support?

No, she had to say that had been a bit unexpected.

"Merge our fashion empires. What an idiot," she said aloud.

"Whatever you say," the cabbie returned in a thick Brooklyn accent.

"Even if I *had* a fashion empire, why would I want to merge it with a guy via a marriage contract? I mean, they have regular contracts for that kind of stuff."

"Sure they do."

"And since I'm not even sure I want to have sex with him, I see absolutely no benefit to me. I mean, isn't that what marriage is all about—regular and sure-thing sex?"

"Not in my house."

Another hit to marriage. She'd seen her sister settle into her happy, domestic life, but sex never seemed at the top of her list. There was the house, the kids, the laundry and the carpool. And her husband seemed just as hurried, trying to advance at his job and earn enough to keep his family comfortable and happy.

None of it was easy. Yet they managed. They loved each other, and they managed. Lily admired them, even as she doubted her life would ever be that balanced.

"Can you believe that man! He actually *proposed*."

The cabbie shook his head. "I'll be damned, lady. You just can't trust anybody these days."

"Hear, hear. And he's not the first! Last year this doctor I was dating proposed that I marry him, move to Connecticut and have six kids together."

"Men are pigs."

Lily stared out the window at the passing city lights, the people streaming past the shops, the crush of cabs and limos outside the hotels. Damn, she loved New York. Full of crazy men, but still the best.

"Here ya go," the cabbie said as he pulled up to the curb in front of her building.

"Thanks."

The doorman opened the cab's door and greeted her with a dignified nod.

Lily paid the cabbie and tossed in an extra twenty. Hardworking cabbies were cool. Designers with an attitude and delusions of matrimony were *not*.

JAMES STARED at Teresa over his menu. "Did you say something?"

"Twice." She smiled. "I asked what you were going to have."

"I'm not sure. Maybe the fish. I'm not really hungry." He set his menu aside and rubbed the bridge of his nose. He couldn't get the look of shock and—dare he say—hurt on Lily's face out of his mind.

To say the least, her reaction was unexpected.

Though she was flamboyant, disorganized and temperamental, she was also smart, savvy and talented. With the money pouring in from her designs, she certainly needed a financial adviser, but a decent secretary could handle her appointments and the office work.

She didn't need someone like him to hold her hand, get her out of bed in the morning or rescue her from her latest crisis. All things he'd done over and over for past clients.

Maybe, at times, she lacked complete confidence in herself. She had confidence in her work, but not in her ability to multitask, to handle her business, to make the best decisions. But he saw all those qualities in her. And more.

As a man, he couldn't deny her physical presence—bright green eyes, long legs, black hair and toned figure. But her temper, all-night parties, spontaneity to the point of head-spinning craziness, flashy personality and—had he listed her fiery temper?—had him shaking his head. Too much like his mother and her wild actor friends, the people he'd known from childhood, but never understood or felt comfortable with. A business-casual distance from Lily was a necessity for him.

Client she was. And client she'd stay.

"James?"

James blinked at Teresa. He had the feeling she'd called his name more than once. He reached across the table and squeezed her hand—just as he'd done to Lily earlier.

Get her out of your mind, buddy. The workday is done. Thank God.

"I'm sorry," he said to Teresa. *She* was the kind of woman he belonged with, the kind of woman who wanted a quiet, normal life. "I had a wild day at work, and I'm having a hard time setting the details aside."

"I saw several pairs of Lily's shoes at Blooming-dale's the other day. They were really...colorful."

"That's Lily."

Teresa smiled, and pushed a strand of her blond bob behind her ear. "A second-grade schoolteacher doesn't have much use for four-inch stilettos, I'm afraid."

"I wouldn't think that's a bad thing. They look really uncomfortable to me."

The waitress appeared with their drinks, then took their orders. James ate in this casual restaurant down the street from his apartment often. He liked the worn tables, open-air kitchen, simple food. Others obviously agreed with him, he thought, noting the entryway crowded with people waiting for tables.

After a sip of wine, James admitted, "I told Lily about my retirement today."

"Ah. I guess she didn't take it well."

"No."

"She relies on you. She probably feels you're abandoning her."

"I thought she'd throw things at me."

"And she cried instead?"

He angled his head. How did other women know this kind of stuff about each other? Teresa and Lily had never met; they were as unalike as two women could be. Were there Cliff Notes somewhere? Maybe a course? "She was upset."

"Give her some time. She'll accept it and move on—without missing a beat, I'll bet."

Well, he wouldn't mind if she missed him a *little*. Even if he had begun his career with reluctance, he'd gotten pretty damn good at it.

But not for much longer. Soon he'd only have himself to worry about. Himself and maybe a family of his own.

He could envision Teresa embracing retirement with him. His culinary classes. His marketing studies on the latte business. She'd also fit in well with his horses, or maybe dog breeding. She'd enjoy helping him run a café. And his life would finally be regular like everybody else's.

"You're right. She'll be fine without me."

"People like Lily always come out on top."

She made the comment without any jealousy or anger. Graciousness. Wasn't that an ideal quality in a mate? "They do indeed. Mostly because she's determined that's where she belongs." Considering, James sipped his wine. "It's kind of an odd mix of willpower and ego."

"From the descriptions you've given me, she seems really...flashy."

"Oh, she is. She certainly fits in much better with my parents' theater friends than I do."

Smiling, Teresa nodded. "Your parents are very flamboyant, too."

"Especially Mother."

"But entertaining. The night I met them at that party, and your mother and her friend reenacted the entire final scene of a play they did ten years ago? Amazing. She was obviously born to her craft."

He liked talking with Teresa. They were friends, and their relationship was comfortable. With his parents' volatile marriage as his first impression of life-time commitment, he'd figured out really early that was not what he wanted for himself. He didn't need impulsiveness and all-consuming passion. Flames like that burned out—or burned each other up. He'd seen it happen over and over again among his parents' friends.

Before he could respond to Teresa, someone called his name.

He turned to see his good friend and lawyer, Dalton Roberts, approaching their table with a slinky blonde clinging to his arm.

Dalton had moved to Manhattan from South Carolina several years ago after his law practice had fallen apart. His partner and his wife had had an affair that devastated him, so now he was a confirmed bachelor and play-the-field guy.

Actually, he and Lily were very alike. If James didn't have a strict aversion to playing matchmaker with friends and business associates—between anybody, really—he'd encourage them to go out.

He rose and introduced his buddy to Teresa, then was introduced to Dalton's date, Cindy. James appreciated Teresa's ability to send the new woman a welcoming smile and stare into her eyes rather than at her chest. Dalton tended to go for flash over substance in choosing women, but Cindy and her well-endowed figure was a new, uh…high.

The waitress appeared to offer the new guests

drinks, and James encouraged them to hang out until their own table was ready. With his longish blond hair and quick smile, Dalton was "dreamy" and easy to talk to, according to the female population. Teresa might as well meet his friends.

"So, how's business?" Dalton asked James.

"Good. Spring is a big season for us." Actually, he'd told Dalton he'd get him near-the-front seats for the Spectacular—he was sure his friend would enjoy checking out the models—but he didn't want to say so in front of Cindy. He expected his buddy would want to come solo.

Dalton took a sip of the whiskey the waitress brought, then grinned. "Any woman who showed up at my door wearing those high-assed shoes I saw in that ad on Fifth… Whoa, baby."

The ad was provocative—showing a woman from behind, wearing no top as she smiled teasingly over her shoulder and dressed in a short, black skirt, fishnets and a pair of Lily's red stilettos.

Cindy leaned forward, and James feared they all might get to know her a little too familiarly if she made that motion then drew a deep breath. "*You're* the one who works for *Lily Reaves?*"

She said Lily's name with the same breathy quality he'd witnessed in countless women the last several months. Women apparently worshiped shoes with the same fervor as men worshiped sports. Or women.

"She makes the most *amazing* shoes," Cindy continued. "I've got on a pair now, in fact." She lifted her leg above the table, obviously intending to show everyone, but Dalton tamped her down.

James exchanged a look with Teresa, who grinned

at him and shrugged. Their quiet dinner was turning into a sideshow, with Lily being the topic of conversation. Gracious didn't even begin to cover the woman's positive qualities.

Yep, she'd fit into his plans perfectly.

3

BACK IN HER APARTMENT, but still dressed in her Brian-the-disastrous-date pantsuit, Lily punched in Gwen's cell-phone number. "I need you," she said without ceremony.

"*Now?* We're at the Tiger, Lil."

"I know."

"I just saw some big-time rapper."

"Who?"

"Don't know his name, but he ordered champagne for the entire bar, so that qualifies as cool in my book." She paused, slurping. "What's up?"

"James is retiring. Brian proposed."

Silence. Then, "That doesn't sound good."

"Duh! I'm officially having a pity party. Where are *you?*"

"I'm having a free freakin' glass of champagne."

"I'm drinking alone."

"I'm now draining said glass and signaling Kristin. We're on our way." Her voice became muffled, then she came back clearer. "Any particular reason for retirement or proposal?"

"James wants to open a café in Connecticut. Brian thinks I'm a vulnerable woman who needs his protection."

"I won't even touch the vulnerable-woman thing, 'cause that's just stupid, but what the hell is so interesting about Connecticut?"

"Exactly my reaction."

"Okay, hang on. We're on our way."

By the time they arrived, Lily had pulled cold pizza from the fridge again and was drinking chardonnay straight out of the bottle. She leaned against the door and let her friends in the apartment.

"Give me that!" Kristin said, snatching the bottle. "For God's sake, you can at least use a glass."

Lily sniffled. "Why? My life is over."

Gwen grabbed her arm, dragged her over to the couch, then pulled her down and sat beside her. "Stay."

Lily slid her arm from her friend's grasp and was about to shove another bite of pizza in her mouth when Gwen grabbed that, too. Man, that woman was tough. She had a reputation for tough, and Lily knew better than anybody just how truly deserved it was.

She, Gwen and Kristin had met about five years ago at a women's business seminar. They'd all been out of school for a few years—Lily from the fashion institute, Gwen from NYU and Kristin from the Pink Petal School of Hair and Cosmetology. Lily had been working for a top designer at the time, but he never let her share her creativity or have any input into the designs. The others had had similar experiences, so, frustrated working for other people, each of them had decided to open her own business—and had absolutely no idea what the hell they were doing.

Over the years they'd shared ideas, triumphs and setbacks in both their business and personal lives.

Lily was more grateful for their friendship than just about anything.

Kristin brought glasses, the wine bottle and ice bucket into the den, arranging everything on the coffee table. Then, when she saw the pizza, sent Gwen into the kitchen for a decent snack.

Sitting cross-legged on the floor next to the sofa, Kristin stared at Lily. "Let's start with Brian."

She huffed out a breath. "Why? I don't care about Brian." How whiny could she get? She hated how this was affecting her so adversely, but, damn, she really hadn't seen a day this awful coming.

"But maybe I'll understand a little better how you got in this state," Kristin said.

Gwen—her tall, thin body encased in a spectacular bronze dress, her dark hair pulled up loose and sexy on her head—shoved aside a stack of magazines, then set a plate of grapes and cheese on the coffee table. Lily's gaze shifted to Kristin—a voluptuous blonde, who wore a body-skimming pale pink pantsuit.

She'd really messed up her friends' night out. Since they looked as great as they did, she felt doubly guilty. "I shouldn't have dragged you guys over here."

Kristin waved her hand. "Forget it. We weren't having that good a time, anyway."

As she was settling on the other end of the sofa, Gwen opened her mouth, looking as if she might argue, but bit into a grape instead.

"So, Gwen told me Brian thought you were vulnerable and that's why he proposed."

"What I want to know," Gwen said, "is whether

you kneed him in the balls or ground your stiletto into his foot."

Lily tossed back her hair. "Neither. I showed great restraint."

Kristin grinned. "That's a first."

"He also said I needed a partner who'd support and understand me." Lily frowned. "I've got James. What do I need with a partner?"

Kristin pursed her lips. "He probably meant an emotional partner, someone to share your life with."

Lily waved her hand in dismissal. "I'm not ready for a commitment like that. Besides, I've got friends."

"What about sex?" Gwen asked.

Lily gulped her wine. "According to my cabbie, marriage isn't a guarantee of that, either." And she was going to give her sister hell about that the next time they talked. She'd never felt as though she fit in with her conservative, country-loving family, though she'd never all out said she was against something as basic to human life as marriage. But this whole lack-of-sex thing had her reassessing.

"My cousin says the same thing," Kristin added. "Says she and her husband never do it anymore."

"I wasn't that interested in Brian, anyway," Lily said, then, sighing—the whole deal really was pretty embarrassing—she recounted her conversation with Brian, including his revelation that he wanted a sugar mama.

Kristin shook her head in disgust. "Men are whacked."

"It's no wonder we're not all married and knocked up on a regular basis," Gwen said dryly.

Lily raised her eyebrows, the picture of a blown-up Gwen zipping laughingly before her eyes. "*You* pregnant? Ha!"

"Maybe someday," Gwen said.

"You're not very maternal, girl," Kristin pointed out.

"You kill plants," Lily said.

"And pets," Kristin added.

"*One* fish." Eyes narrowed, Gwen raised her finger. "One lousy, stupid beta fish, and you guys think I'm a killer."

"Well, you can't deny your place is a grave for any kind of fern, ivy or ficus tree," Lily said.

"I can't help it if people keep giving them to me." She pointed at Lily. "In fact, *you* gave me the last green thing."

"Along with fertilizer and very specific instructions. I still don't know how you managed to kill it in less than a week."

"I would have thrown myself off the balcony the first day," Kristin said without meeting Gwen's gaze. "Less suffering that way."

Gwen crossed her arms over her chest. "Since when did this become a 'let's pick on Gwen' party?" She snapped her fingers. "Let's get back on topic, people."

Lily pushed out her lip. "I don't want to talk about Brian anymore."

"I agree," Kristin said. "What a jerk."

"Then we move on to James." Gwen met Lily's gaze. "How much time have you got?"

"Three months."

"Three months! What happened to giving two weeks' notice?"

"James plans ahead," Lily said. And she didn't. Yet

another reason she absolutely couldn't let him go. She really wished she could set aside the clawing fear that she was going to fall flat on her face if James left, but the dread in the pit of her stomach just wouldn't subside.

"Okay, so we've got some time to convince him to stay," Kristin said.

Gwen kicked off her shoes and tucked her feet beneath her. "Just sleep with him."

Kristin toasted Gwen with her half-empty wineglass. "Sounds like a plan. He's dreamy."

Lily stared down at her friend. "Dreamy? *James?*"

Kristin batted her lashes. "He's got great eyes."

"And a great ass," Gwen added.

Had she been asleep for the last nine months? "Since when are you two checking out my assistant?"

Gwen smiled. "Since the moment he got here."

Lily fluffed up the pillow behind her head. "I'm *not* sleeping with him." Not that James was completely un-sleep-with material. She just didn't think a) he'd go for it, or b) that he'd be fooled for a second by her sudden amorousness. "I could throw a fit."

Kristin giggled. "I bet you already did that."

"I might have raised my voice," Lily said indignantly, even as Gwen snorted with laughter. "But Connecticut, Kris! Why would anyone want to live in *Connecticut?*"

"It's peaceful and elegant. Lots of nice estates and quaint towns."

"I guess they have some great restaurants," Gwen said. "You can get a kick-butt chowder—"

"You two are *not* helping."

"What have you got against a whole state?" Gwen

asked, reaching over to pull the wine from the ice bucket.

"They...they have...cows."

Gwen rolled her eyes.

"How about I come up with a list of cons for why he shouldn't leave? James is into lists."

Kristin pursed her lips. "Hmm. Like what?" She patted Lily's leg. "Other than the obvious fact that he's losing you."

"The pulse and excitement of the city, for one," Lily said.

"But you said he wants peace and quiet," Gwen reminded her.

"We have peace in the city," Lily said. "What the hell do you think Central Park's for?"

"And the Met," Kristin added. "Culture, refinement, tourists whispering and pointing at the Van Goghs." She paused. "Okay, maybe not."

Lily glared at her friends. "*Hel-lo!* The theater, the clubs, the restaurants, the shopping, Bloomingdale's, Tiffany, Henri Bendel—"

"I sincerely doubt James will mourn the loss of Henri Bendel," Gwen said.

"Cosmetics and accessories are probably not his thing," Kristin agreed.

But Lily grinned. "I've got it. The Yankees."

Gwen shivered. "Oooh, Derek Jeter."

"James is a *huge* Yankee fan," Lily continued. "I bought him season tickets for his birthday. The games are practically the only time he takes off, and if he can't go, he follows them on the radio or Internet. Yankee Stadium is quite a commute from Connecticut."

Kristin gestured with her glass. "Oh, that's good.

Love these, by the way." She picked up the silver sandal Lily had kicked off earlier.

Tears burned in Lily's throat. "I'll never design another pair once he leaves."

Gwen tossed a pillow at her. "Get real, girl."

Kristin set the shoe aside, then met Lily's gaze. "Are you sure losing your assistant is all that you're worked up about?"

"It's not like he plays a minor role in my life."

Kristin and Gwen exchanged a glance. "Are you sure his business expertise is the only thing you're worried about losing?" Kristin asked.

"What else would I be worried about losing?"

"What Kristin is trying—and not too well—to ask you is...do you have the hots for him?"

Those two had lost their minds. The hots for *James?* The man who thought wearing a beige shirt instead of a white one was a fashion risk? The man who probably organized his sock drawer? As an assistant, she wouldn't have anybody else. As a potential lover, forget it. "Of course I don't have the hots for him. Where in the world did you get that idea?"

"You're really messed up about this," Kristin said gently.

"Well, *yeah.* I'm worried my business is going to go down the drain!"

"That's all?" Gwen pressed.

"Isn't that enough?"

Kristin angled her head. "I don't know. I think you might be making a mistake. James is..."

"Smart," Gwen said.

"Responsible," Kristin said.

"Loyal."

"Dreamy."

Lily folded her arms across her chest. "My assistant."

"Not for much longer," her friends said in unison.

"Please stop," Lily said dryly. "You're cheering me up way too much." She reached for the wine, pouring the last few drops into her glass. A bit woozy, she rose and headed to the fridge for another bottle. As she refilled everyone's glasses, she considered her strategy with James. He would respond to a logical list of pros and cons—though without the pros, since she didn't want him to leave. But she needed a backup. He would probably find a way to argue around her cons. She hadn't succeeded in moving him an inch earlier.

She paced the den. "Maybe I could sue him. For canceling our contract or something."

"But you said he's finishing his contract," Gwen said.

Kristin shook her head. "Oh, that's good. Kill him with kindness."

Lily stopped and smiled for the first time all night. "That's it!" James didn't realize how much she needed him. He didn't know how grateful she was that he'd done so much for her business. She had a tendency to be single-minded, and the designs for the Spectacular had taken up so much of her energies. She'd neglected her most valuable employee. As she'd learned so long ago at the women's business seminar, that was a big no-no.

"I haven't complimented him enough," she went on. "I haven't let him know how much I appreciate him."

Kristin set down her wineglass with a click. "You

could wine and dine him. Bring him gifts, little treats with his coffee breaks."

"And what about a raise?" Gwen added.

Kristin frowned. "Don't you think that's a bit obvious?"

"Since when is Lily ever subtle?"

"Stop nagging," Lily said, planting her hands on her hips. "And help me think of a plan."

EARLY THE NEXT MORNING, as James was answering his e-mail, Lily appeared in his office with a cookie—one of those giant chocolate-chip ones with lots of icing that formed mostly illegible letters of white goo. *Thonk Yau* was written on the top.

"You shouldn't have."

James marveled that with bloodshot eyes, Lily still managed to beam as she set the box on his desk. "Just wanted to let you know you were appreciated."

That was his Lily—subtle down to the tips of her hot-pink, patent-leather ankle boots.

He tore off a small piece and offered it to her. She curled her lip, and laid her hand across her stomach. "It's a bit early for me."

Striving for polite, but suspicious as hell of her motives, James popped the cookie in his mouth. After swallowing, he asked, "Late night?"

Guilt skittered across her face. "A bit."

What exactly had she done on this date?

"Actually, I got back early from my date and called Gwen and Kristin."

Ah. The three divas. He wondered how late into the night they'd slammed him. Besides being completely loyal to Lily and probably not liking him messing with her world, none of them could appreciate his need for peace and quiet.

So how had they gone from condemning him to Lily bringing him a cookie?

"How was your date?" she asked.

"Nice."

"Nice?"

He leaned back in his chair, noting her expression had soured even further. "Something wrong with nice?"

She angled her head. "Well, yeah—" She stopped and set her jaw, then made an obvious effort to smile. "No, no. Of course not."

"Are you going to tackle the drawings for the rhinestone sandals today?"

"I thought I'd help you, actually."

"Help me?" Oh, yeah, Lily was up to something. "With what?"

"I could file things. Or straighten up your office."

James glanced around the pristine room. His desk calendar was lined up precisely with the edge of his desk. His pencils and pens were all turned point down in their brass holder. His computer, desk and credenza were free of dust. "You want to file and clean?"

She smiled. "You're worth it. You deserve the best."

"Uh-huh." He'd bet his Yankee season tickets that she and her friends had cursed his name, then plotted the best way to keep him around. A completely transparent plan of action, but he had to admit he was a little surprised she'd decided to start with flattery. He would have put money on an angry tirade first.

She crossed to him. "Are you stressed? I could rub your shoulders."

"I don't think—"

Too late. Lily slid her hands onto his shoulders and squeezed.

He craned his head around to look at her. "What are you—"

Oh, wow. That actually felt good. No, bad. In fact, he didn't like that rubbing, warmth, pressing and smoothing at all.

He valued his decisiveness and professionalism. A massage by your boss could never be listed under professional office decorum.

She pressed her thumbs against the back of his shoulders.

Unable to help himself, he closed his eyes. He should make her stop. He should call a halt to this whole, too-friendly encounter. Of course, she couldn't possibly mean anything sexual by her actions.

She wasn't the type of woman he was attracted to, and he felt certain she thought the same about him. From what he'd seen, she liked men with way more flash and charm than him. She'd never treated him like anything but an employee and business confidant—though he did think they'd become friends over the last several months. As a friend, he could care about her and her business, but not cross that line of getting too involved in her life.

Besides, she wasn't part of his plan. He was going to quietly finish his contract, leaving Lily to her parties, creative bursts of energy, crazy friends and chaos. His goal of a normal life, the life he was *supposed* to be leading, didn't include a woman like Lily.

She moved to his neck, her delicate fingers sending a ripple of pleasure down his spine. Okay, this really had gone too—

Garnet burst into the office. "Oh, God, I *knew* I smelled chocolate."

Lily jumped away from James, and reality thankfully slammed him back to his senses.

Garnet's gaze bounced around until it locked on to the cookie. She used her long, gold fingernail to cut herself a large piece, then plopped her butt on James's desk. "Oh, that's good," she moaned as she chewed.

"Come on in, Garnet," Lily said, tapping her foot. "Make yourself at home. Have some cookie."

"Can't hear you. My taste buds are having an orgasm."

For once, James was actually *glad* to see Garnet. He straightened his tie and shoved that unproductive moment of pleasure with Lily aside. "You know, I was working before you two interrupted."

Lily poked out her bottom lip. "You don't like the cookie?"

"The cookie is *fabulous*," Garnet said.

"Yes, I like the cookie." He really was going to miss that adorable face of hers. But she shouldn't be a central figure in his life. He didn't belong in the fashion industry. Personally, he liked a nice suit as much as the next guy, but this constant obsession over shoes and dresses you wore one time with impractical handbags that held nothing made him want to throw his hands in the air. "But I don't *need* the cookie."

"Everyone should be aware of their value to a company."

"I feel like I'm rolling around in the diamond case at Cartier."

Patience obviously spent, Lily glared at Garnet, who didn't bother to stop moaning over the cookie to notice. Lily shifted her attention back to him. "And you are the most valuable member of this company."

"Then why isn't *my* name on the front door?" he couldn't help but tease.

"Is that what you want? I could—"

"No, Lily, that's not what I want."

Garnet raised her hand. "I do."

"Garnet, *please*," Lily said.

James wasn't reveling in Lily's frustration—even though the bribing-with-a-cookie thing was a little underhanded—but neither did he want Lily to send Garnet out. He suspected the receptionist was the only thing standing between him and Lily and another dead-end conversation about his retirement.

Or another massage.

"I'm glad you appreciate me, Lily, but you don't need cookies."

"I—" Garnet began before Lily cut her off.

"I just want you to feel fulfilled in your job."

He couldn't very well say he was. That was the whole point of this change in his life. He was meant for something other than this manager-of-chaos role he'd fallen into. Culinary school or business school? With café owner somewhere in between, it sounded like nirvana. "You're definitely my favorite client." Of course the others had been spoiled, temperamental shrews.

And that was just the men.

He rose. "Okay, ladies. Break's over. Let's get back to work."

Garnet grabbed the cookie box and held it against her chest. "I'll go but this is going with me."

Lily grabbed the box and tugged. "That cookie belongs to James. Give it back."

Garnet yanked the box back toward her. "I've worked here four whole months and no one gave *me* a cookie. I want this one."

Growling, Lily tugged harder. "You can't have it."

James shook his head. One normal day. He wanted just one normal day at the office. "Ladies!"

They stopped tugging but continued to glare at each other over the box.

"How about we cut the cookie in half? I don't mind sharing."

Lily nodded and stepped back, allowing him to take the box. Since Garnet had pigged out, there really wasn't much cookie left, but knowing the women were watching, he took great care to cut two even pieces—with his polished brass letter opener, no less.

After the door was finally closed behind those two, he sank into his chair. From his desk drawer, he pulled out the small calendar he'd bought. He had a big black X through Monday. He visualized the moment he could cross out today and felt calmer.

Lily was proud and independent. Though gracious—except when under extreme pressure—she didn't usually waste time fawning over people. She took everyone at their own value and didn't focus too much on obvious flattery. Surely this *appreciation* wouldn't last long.

James put the whole incident out of his mind and dived back into his work, returning phone calls and discussing with the other designers' assistants the plans for the Spectacular. Though a rental company was providing the runway and seating, they'd decided to build their own sets as a backdrop for the show. But the other assistants just wanted to send a check and let him handle the details. What else was new?

He agreed to be in charge of the project and hung up the phone, wondering if he'd just been manipulated or expedient.

Rap, rap, rap. "James…"

"Come in," he called, bracing himself for Lily's entrance. He should have known she wouldn't retreat for long.

She breezed in, a broad smile on her face, wearing an off-the-shoulder pale pink shirt and a black mini, *mini*skirt that definitely did *not* cover her lower half.

Though she'd certainly worn miniskirts to the office many times, and he *should* have been long immune to both her outrageous behavior and wardrobe, he—well, he stared.

What happened to the T-shirt and jeans she'd worn earlier?

"Hi," she said.

"Hi," he mumbled, whipping his head around to focus on his computer screen.

He sensed her moving closer, then hopping up on his desk.

I am not going to look at her. This is ridiculous. I've worked with her every day for almost a year.

"How about taking a break for lunch?"

"Maybe later." *Don't look over.*

She leaned close. He smelled her perfume—a spicy, elusive fragrance a designer friend made especially for her. "I ordered in from Angelo's."

He looked over.

And nearly swallowed his tongue. A mile of Lily's slender legs dangled off the edge of his desk. And hadn't she mentioned food came with those legs? Nirvana, indeed.

"I ordered your favorite," she said softly, teasingly.

He glanced up, meeting her mischievous green gaze. "Shrimp linguine?"

"Yep."

"I, uh…" He dropped his gaze to her legs again. Sweat broke out on his forehead. What was wrong with him? Why was she affecting him like this? "Okay."

"I've been thinking about what you said earlier. About your name on the door." She looked down at him. "I could make you a partner."

Relieved to focus on something besides yards of smooth-looking skin, he sighed. "Lily, I don't want my name on your door. I want my name on my own door. I'm not a designer, and you're not serious about that offer."

She shrugged. "Maybe not. You know, I understand your need to have your own business, to be in charge of your own destiny. I wanted those things, too. And now that I have them, I'll never give them up. But understanding and accepting are two different things." She crossed her arms over her chest. "I really think you're making a big mistake. I think you'll be miserable in Connecticut."

"I won't."

"What if I decide to prove it to you?"

"I suppose you could try." What was he doing—encouraging her?

Her eyes lit up.

Panic tightened his stomach. "What I meant to say was—"

"You're coming to lunch?"

"I'll be there, but—"

Lily wasn't listening. She slid off the desk, then strutted to the door, and he noted the black sling backs with pink polka dots covering her feet.

Why couldn't she design shoes for Nike? Sneakers were much more practical.

"Don't be long," she said over her shoulder. "It'll get cold."

When she was gone, he slumped in his chair. He tried to remind himself she was bribing him with lunch. And possibly her legs.

He could see right through her plan. None of it would change his mind about leaving. But he was a practical man. A man who thought through his actions before he moved.

So it was with great deliberation that James rushed out of the office after her.

4

LILY SMILED as James leaned back in his chair at the conference table with a satisfied sigh.

He'd practically inhaled his linguine, and she'd done a very nice job of keeping the conversation centered around regular work stuff and not his retirement. She was going to finesse his surrender, not nag it into happening. A woman who'd made it from a farm in Iowa to New York City did not sit around and cry, waiting for what she wanted to come along.

"What about an arch in the background?"

Lazily, he glanced her way. His eyes were soft and unfocused. "Arch?"

"For the Spectacular. At one end of the runway. It could be a bridge from winter to spring."

He straightened immediately and glanced around as if he'd forgotten where he was. She was sorry she'd spoken so soon. He was rarely still and relaxed. He'd actually looked pretty cute. Maybe even sexy.

She shook her head to clear her thoughts. Maybe she was still under the Linguine Stupor, too. Because James was cute, definitely cute. But sexy? No way. No how. Gwen and Kristin had done this to her with their absurd "you've got the hots for him" ideas.

"An arch sounds good," he said, pushing aside his plate and pulling his PDA from his shirt pocket.

"And can we put lights on it?"

"Lights," he repeated, making a note.

The canned lights over the table seemed to focus on him, accenting strands of golden brown mixed among the dark. How had she never noticed those contrasts before?

Because it doesn't matter what color his hair is as long as he keeps the office running. Get a grip, girl.

She leaned back in her chair, staring at the ceiling. "Should we run the lights around the arch? Or maybe we could dangle them from the top."

"Maybe both."

"And we need lots of plants and flowers in the background. Everyone's collection is full of bright colors."

"Fine, but we should go with silk in case anyone has allergies."

"I guess it wouldn't be good for the models to sneeze down the runway."

"A good sneeze would blow some of those models *off* the runway."

She grinned at him. "Funny." He wasn't an uptight conservative *all* the time. He appealed to *some* woman, after all. "What does this woman you're seeing look like?" she asked before she caught herself.

He glanced up from his notepad. "Attractive blonde, average height, blue eyes. Why?"

Geez. What a romantic. She'd asked what she looked like, not for the description on her driver's license. "I was trying to picture you with a tall, skinny model type and couldn't. Is she smart?" If a woman could be turned on by brains, then James was an ideal match.

"She's intelligent. Can we get back to the set now?"

Lily waved her hand. "Of course. Sorry. I think I was up too late last night."

"We want lights on the runway, right?"

"Oh, yeah. Plenty of spotlights. What about different-colored ones? That would be a good thing for spring."

He shook his head. "It will mess up publicity photos. We have dozens of fashion magazine reporters and photographers coming. We need strong, simple lighting. Let the designs be the color."

This was the kind of thing he excelled at. When she got carried away with an idea, he always reminded her what was important. He kept his focus.

Simple, he would say. Something anybody could do. But she knew better. She needed him to bounce ideas off, someone she trusted, someone who excelled in areas that she didn't.

"Lily?" Garnet's voice floated out of the intercom. "They're here."

Finally. She was depressing herself with all this negativity and worry over James. She sprung from her chair. "Now for the fun part," she said as she pulled two high-backed, beige leather conference chairs away from the table.

James eyed her suspiciously. "What fun?"

Lily beamed. "I arranged for us to have a manicure and pedicure—right here in the office."

"A mani—" He shook his head. "No. Absolutely not."

"Oh, they're fabulous. Have you ever had one?"

He stood. "No, and I know I don't want one."

She pushed him back into his chair. "Oh, yes, you do. You deserve to be pampered."

Kristin had assured her men got manicures, and while James was conservative and restrained at times, he was always impeccably groomed.

As the door opened, James actually paled and rose from his chair. "I'm not taking off my shoes in the office."

Lily planted her hands on her hips. "Oh, good grief."

She spun away from him and greeted Marla and Samantha, the two manicurists from Kristin's hair and nail spa. "He's a virgin," she said, jerking her thumb over her shoulder to indicate James. "Be gentle."

Lily helped the women roll their mini jet baths across the room, kicked off her shoes, then plopped down in one of the chairs.

"Lily, can I talk to you?" James asked in a strained voice, still standing next to the conference table.

As Marla picked up her bare foot and placed it in the bubbling water, Lily patted the chair next to her. "That's the beauty of all this. We can continue our meeting and still have our treatments at the same time." She smiled widely. "Efficient, yes?"

James eyed Samantha and her minibath with distinct distrust.

With their white lab coats and rubber-soled shoes, Marla and Samantha looked more like nurses than technicians in a girlie-girl salon. Lily honestly didn't get it. Was this a man thing? Or just a James thing? She wanted to pamper him, show him that working for her in the city didn't have to be all rush, rush, stress, stress.

"Come on. Samantha doesn't care if you have ugly feet."

That got him moving. "I don't have ugly feet," he said as he started, albeit slowly, toward them.

"Prove it."

He muttered and glared, but he finally—after untying his shoelaces, folding his socks and precisely placing them inside his shoes—sat in the chair next to her. "Happy?"

"Immensely." She leaned forward, checking out his feet. "Not bad. Cute toes."

He turned bright red. "This isn't normal, Lily. Normal office procedures do not involve manicures and pedicures."

"Well, they damn well should."

Closing his eyes, he leaned his head back against the chair. "One normal day. Is that too much to ask for?"

Lily patted his knee. "Would you relax? Nobody's going to paint your toes pink or anything." Then, laughing, she winked at Samantha.

IN STARBUCKS a few days later, Lily sipped her cappuccino and waited for Fedora. Since James's mother was forever late, she figured she had a good twenty minutes of brainstorming time.

She liked the sketches of the rhinestone sandals she'd been working on, but still felt as if something was missing. Maybe instead of alternating yellow and clear stones, she should go with all clear. Or maybe blue. She had lots of yellow in the collection, but little in blue.

But would shoe buyers stress out over matching the blue exactly to whatever they wanted to wear?

She knew she would. Still, she wanted color. Was color "normal"?

Frustrated by her indecision, she shoved her coffee aside. She wished she could blame her troubles on too much caffeine, but she knew the cause—she'd gotten dependent on James helping her talk through the creative process. She'd gotten used to him rattling off statistics, cost ratios and industry trends.

And her mind wouldn't stay focused on rhinestones and shoes. James's words about a "normal" day kept invading her thoughts.

They had normal days every day. They came to work, made coffee, answered phones, accomplished stuff, had lunch, accomplished more stuff, talked on the phone some more, then went home. What was abnormal about *that*?

But, obviously, something was wrong. Once James had given in, she thought he'd enjoyed the manicure and pedicure, but clearly the whole thing had thrown him for a loop. She wondered if she'd taken a giant step back instead of making progress.

"Hi, Lily, sorry I'm late." Dressed in a plum-colored pantsuit, Fedora plopped into the chair opposite her. Her smile was bright but her eyes tired. "We had a late rehearsal last night—the director wanted to change five lines, and somehow that threw everybody off."

"They're just not as professional as you."

Fedora waved her hand. "They're just not as experienced as me. I'm an old dog at this game."

Lily raised her eyebrows. "You're not an old dog."

Fedora sighed. "Oh, yes, I am."

Since they met a couple times a month for coffee

or lunch and had become good friends in the process, Lily knew something wasn't right with Fedora.

"What's up?" she asked, pinning Fedora with her gaze.

"I'm just old."

"You are *not*." Lily was so shocked by the gloomy expression on Fedora's face, she laid her hand on her arm. "You're talented and lovely."

Fedora shook her head. "My life is a big yawn. Yours is exciting. You're free to go wherever, do whatever you want."

"Martin is holding you prisoner in midtown?"

Fedora laughed. "Oh, Lily, I'm so glad to have you as a friend. You get right to the point. And I don't know what's wrong with me. Martin drives me crazy sometimes, but still, he's mine. I just feel at odds with everything."

Could this depression be about James and his retirement? Lily hadn't spoken to Fedora since her assistant's big announcement, and she hesitated to do so now. It was one thing to plot ways to keep James in the city with her other friends, but another thing entirely to do so with a friend who just happened to be his mother.

Before she could press her for more details, Fedora's cell phone rang. In a matter of moments, Fedora was apologizing for a late appointment and rushing out of the coffee shop.

Alone again and frustrated with her own troubles, Lily tried to focus on rhinestones. She even pulled out her pocketbook sketch pad, but no clear answer would come. She scowled out the window beside her table as a sea of businesspeople, tourists and sophisticated shoppers flew by. Were they normal? Was walking to work normal? She did that every day.

Tossing aside her pencil, she flipped open her phone and called Gwen.

"Gwen, what does a normal office do?"

"Lily, I have programs to write, e-mail to answer and a client screaming about some virus. I don't have time for another crisis."

Lily flung out her hand. "See! Normal means stress and rush, rush. He doesn't want that."

"He?"

"James."

"Ah."

"He wants a normal day. How in the world do I accomplish that?"

Gwen was silent a moment, and Lily almost took back her request. Did she really want to change the office to accommodate James's wishes? Was it really necessary to compromise herself that way?

She looked down at her blank sketch pad. Hell, yes.

"You'll have to get Garnet to help," Gwen said finally.

Lily heaved a big sigh. "If I have to."

"And I think we also need to make some wardrobe modifications."

Lily nearly broke down and cried. She thought she at least had style. "What's wrong with my wardrobe?"

"Nothing for a creative office. But when James says normal, he really means conservative. If you make an effort to make him comfortable, he'll notice, believe me."

Lily pulled her sketch pad toward her. She'd spent

the last several days flattering the man like crazy, maybe this new tactic would at least be a change of pace. "Okay, hit me with it."

"Remember these words—quiet, efficiency, promptness..."

Operation Normal Day began the following morning. Lily hovered by the door connecting her apartment to the office. She heard James come in, then walk down the hall. She tried to picture his surprise and confusion as he discovered a hot and fresh cappuccino—made from the machine he'd given her for Christmas—waiting for him. How long she could keep rushing over there and getting things going, she didn't know. That man got up *early.*

The moment she heard the front door open again, she rushed through the door and tiptoed down the hall, reaching Garnet just as she opened her mouth to yell her greeting of "I'm here!" throughout the office.

Lily grabbed Garnet's hand and led her to her desk. "Pick up the phone, buzz James's office and tell him you're here. Ask him if he needs anything and wish him a good day."

Garnet looked at her as if she'd suddenly sprouted alien antennae on her head. "O-kaay."

While Garnet talked on the phone, Lily hovered. This had better work. Gwen was the best, probably the only "normal" businesswoman she knew. "What did he say?" Lily asked the moment Garnet hung up.

Garnet reached for her purse and began fumbling through it. "Thanks and no and thanks."

"*Garnet...*"

"He said 'thanks' when I told him I was here. He

said 'no' when I asked if he needed anything. He said 'thanks' again when I told him to have a good day."

"But what was his tone? Pleased? Surprised?"

"I don't know. Surprised, maybe."

Lily sat on the edge of the desk. Gwen was a certified genius. Maybe this really would work. "Okay. Here's the plan—today we're going to be normal."

Garnet paused in the act of pulling nail polish from her bag. "Huh? How?"

"Remember yesterday when the manicurists got here and you used the intercom instead of yelling down the hall?"

"Yeah?"

"Stuff like that."

Garnet angled her head, looking at Lily from head to toe. "You're wearing a dark suit and low-heeled shoes."

"I found it in the back of my closet. I think I wore it the day I asked the bank for a loan."

Garnet wrinkled her nose. "Your hair is in a bun."

Lily raised her hand to the top of her head. "Too much?"

"Too ugly."

Lily rounded the desk and looked at herself in the foyer mirror. Okay, maybe the bun had been a bit over the top. She yanked out the pins as she talked. "We can do this. Gwen says we have to be efficient, quiet and prompt."

"Us?"

Lily glared over her shoulder. "Us." Brightening her expression and walking toward the desk, she continued, "Think of yourself as playing a part on a reality TV show. You're the efficient secretary. You're always polite to callers. You transfer them immediately to the correct person. If you're getting coffee or soda, you stop by your boss's office and ask him if he wants some, too. No two- or three-hour lunches. No yelling down the hall. No painting nails."

Garnet's expression could—only by a great stretch of the imagination—be called put upon. "And how long do I have to do this?"

Feeling optimistic—it was early yet—Lily smiled. "Let's start with today and see how it goes."

"And *why* are we doing this?"

Lily hadn't been able to bring herself to tell Garnet about James wanting to retire. It was humiliating for one thing, and she was afraid if she kept saying the words aloud, they would suddenly come true. "Just do it, please." She paused, considering the idea that she needed not just Garnet's participation but her *enthusiastic* participation. "If you make it all day, I'll give you a pair of shoes. Your choice."

Garnet's smile could have lit the room.

LATER THAT AFTERNOON, at Lily's request of precisely five o'clock, James headed to the conference room. In the doorway, he paused and watched Lily and Garnet setting out caviar and champagne. Only those two would consider this a "normal" office break.

He winced as his gaze slid down Lily's figure. That suit was truly awful. It had him recalling the midmorning break.

"I thought you might like a break," Lily said as she set a tray of coffee and croissants on his credenza.

"You're wearing a suit."

She turned back. "I do, every once in a while."

"And low heels."

"Part of my conservative-businesswoman line." She smiled, though she seemed a bit on edge. *"Your idea, remember?"*

He leaned back in his chair. *"You're up to something."*

"Just working."

"You've never brought me coffee on a tray. And what's going on with Garnet? She's polite and transfers calls correctly."

"We're just trying to be more efficient, like a normal office. Isn't that a good thing?"

Actually, it had kind of freaked him out.

He had to admit they'd pulled off the "normal" day he'd asked for. Calls were answered and transferred properly. The intercoms were used instead of yelling down the hall. Lily had dressed appropriately. No miniskirts and four-inch heels with eye-popping patterns and bright colors. No manicure ambushes—though he'd actually found that relaxing, not that he planned to tell her. She hadn't burst into his office with some wild new idea or stormed up and down the hall as she usually did when she was working on a design that didn't look right.

And the whole thing was just *wrong.*

It was difficult to admit this day of people in bad suits, strained expressions and eerie silence could be laid right at his feet. But honesty forced him to claim responsibility.

He didn't want to change Lily. He just wanted to change *his* life. And while he was certain the idea had been to show him he should stay around here, it had only proven with even more certainty that he didn't belong.

"How does it look?" He heard Lily ask Garnet.

Garnet shrugged. "Nice. Classy. James will like it. I'm glad I'm getting some shoes out of all this. Do you have any idea how exhausting it is to talk to those people all day?"

Lily arranged ice in a bowl, then set the jar of caviar in the middle. "*Those people* pay the bills around here, remember."

Garnet tossed her wheat-blond hair over her shoulder. "I know, I know. When do I get my shoes?"

"We'll talk later."

"Well, when we do, I've got some questions." Garnet paused, straightening the tablecloth. "About designing."

"Designing what?"

"You know, shoes. Like the way you do."

Garnet had design ambitions? James was ashamed to say he'd been so busy criticizing her receptionist qualities, he'd never considered the idea.

Lily obviously thought the same thing. She stared at Garnet in disbelief. "You want to design shoes?"

Garnet lifted her chin. "Maybe."

"Okay. I'll set aside some time in the next day or two."

Grinning, Garnet flounced across the room. When she saw him at the door, she adopted her normally cool expression and commented, "You gotta tell me what you did to get her to do all this for you."

James wasn't about to tell her he'd quit, since Garnet would use that as a tactic—

He smiled. "I gave my notice."

Garnet cocked her head. "No kidding?"

"And, Garnet, take off those shoes before you

leave for the day," Lily said, turning and glaring in her direction. "Those are samples that have to go to Carlotta Gambini's office tomorrow."

James noted the orange kitten-heeled shoes on the receptionist's feet.

Garnet huffed out a breath. "There have *got* to be better jobs out there."

"Possibly," James whispered. "I hear Tommy Hilfiger may be hiring."

Garnet's eyes lit up before she rushed off, muttering to herself.

"James." The moment she noticed him, Lily's irritated expression vanished. She smiled serenely and swept her hand over the poshly laden table, accented by a black silk tablecloth scattered with pale rose petals and burning candles.

He frowned again at her outfit. On any other day she and the decorations would have been color-coordinated. Where was her fire, her sass and temper?

"Come have some champagne," she said, holding out a glass.

He crossed to her, deliberately keeping his gaze on her face and not her suit. His hands itched to undo the starched white blouse buttoned up to her neck.

As he accepted the drink, she asked, "What were you and Garnet plotting over there?"

"Oh, nothing."

"She's done a good job today, don't you think?"

She looked so hopeful, he hesitated to dash her dream. But while he didn't want to see the changes in Lily stick, having Garnet actually work had been wonderful. "Well, she didn't leave anybody on hold for so long that they gave up and called your cell."

Lily nodded enthusiastically. "See, maybe she's finally getting the hang of things."

Wincing, James sipped his champagne. "And here I was hoping she'd get bored with us and move on to try to destroy another designer's office." Maybe his nudge to quit would take root. He almost felt as if he should call the Hilfiger camp and warn them.

Remembering Garnet's tendency to invert phone numbers, though, he quickly changed his mind.

Lily pouted—the first sign of the real her he'd seen all day. "You have to admit it's been a very *normal* day."

He bit back any criticism. She'd gone to a lot of trouble for him. "It certainly has. So, what's all this?" he asked as Lily piled sour cream, egg, caviar and chives onto a toast point. "A going-away party?"

"Don't be silly. You're not leaving, yet." She handed him the hors d'oeuvre. "Just wanted to show my appreciation for all your hard work, lately. You know, the Spectacular wouldn't be happening without you. They probably would have given my gig to Jimmy Choo."

"That's not true. They were clamoring to get you."

"You were critical in the negotiations." Again, she pasted that calm, controlled smile on her face. "How did the other designers feel about the arch?"

"They pretty much left everything up to us."

"You mean they dumped all the work on you." She paused and refilled their glasses. "Well, don't worry. I'll be there to help. And this is exactly why I can't live without you. Who else would take on more work and responsibility? You're invaluable, and—"

"It's not going to work, Lily."

She blinked up at him. "What's not going to work?"

As much as he'd enjoyed an efficient and polite Garnet, he couldn't let her do this to herself another day. He couldn't take advantage, or play clueless. "I'm not changing my mind about retiring."

Patience and goodwill obviously exhausted, she stamped her foot. "Why the hell not?"

"I appreciate all the TLC, and especially the normal day, but I'm still leaving in three months. My decision is final."

She paced. And muttered. And looked heavenward, throwing up her hands. Finally, she faced him. "By settle down, do you mean get married? You said you wanted to settle down in Connecticut."

"Sure, I'd like to," he said, wondering what her new tactic would be. Giving up without a good hard fight wasn't in Lily's genes.

She smirked. "Well, you'd better get busy finding your bride. I bet there's not much of a social scene in Connecticut."

"I'm already seeing someone, remember?"

Wide-eyed, she stared at him. "Are things that serious between you two?"

Not really. He'd been taking things slow with Teresa. They hadn't exchanged more than a mild kiss. But she was his type, the kind of woman he was meant to be with. He was sure his feelings for her would deepen the more time they spent together. And he had no desire for any grand, can't-live-without-you passion. Look where that had gotten his parents. "They could be."

She frowned. "Already?"

"Why do you think there won't be much social life in Connecticut?"

"Well, they have cows and…stuff, don't they?"

"Women don't like cows?"

"No."

Smiling, James popped a toast point in his mouth. When she wasn't driving him crazy, she was hilarious. "You didn't like growing up with cows on the farm?"

"No. As you well know, I didn't."

"I think cows are kind of cute."

She wrinkled her nose. "They're smelly and slow. They're not real bright or particularly useful—except medium rare with a baked potato." She paused. "Maybe they are a little cute when they give you those doe eyes when you feed them, but—" She sliced her hand through the air. "You're a confirmed urbanite. *You* won't like them, or know what to do with them."

"How about if I get a dog? Women can't resist a man and a cute puppy, right?"

"I guess it depends on the dog," she said slowly, her forehead furrowing in annoyance. "You know, the Yankees don't play in Connecticut, not even for away games."

"I can come into the city for games occasionally." He was going to miss the short commute to the stadium, but he could always buy one of those big plasma screens that made the game look better from your living room than it did live. He'd adapt.

"And what about the shopping up there? How are you going to get those snazzy suits of yours?"

"What do I need snazzy suits for on a farm?"

"I suppose you're going to wear overalls."

"I wouldn't say that."

She stalked two steps forward, her hands planted

on her hips. "Restaurants. Where are you going to eat? Get top-notch Chinese takeout? What about *Angelo's*?"

Shrugging, he sipped champagne. "I hear they have great chowder."

She jutted her face toward his. They were almost nose to nose. "*Chowder?*" she whispered. "I give you Angelo's, and all you can say is chowder?"

"I—" She really smelled…nice. Those green sparks shooting from her eyes were kind of…interesting. And he was at work, not a cocktail party.

He backed up. "I'm really going to miss these little talks of ours, Lily."

"Oohh!" She stormed around the room, reminding him that her temperament and his could only mix for limited moments of time. "When you're craving linguine don't come crying to me. I won't help you. I won't!"

"I won't deserve your help." He hated upsetting her like this. He admitted he hadn't anticipated feeling this bad, this guilty. But he reminded himself that she didn't really need him. She'd realize that once she calmed down.

Sometime next year.

Suddenly, she sank into a chair. "You can't do this, James. I can't make it without you."

He set his glass on the table and knelt in front of her. True worry made her eyes gloomy and lackluster.

Jerk. Louse. Look what you've done to her.

He shook aside his conscience. Lily's sadness wouldn't last long. She always came out on top. She was just shocked and off balance. "*You* can do anything," he said.

She played with the stem of her champagne glass.

"I'm not good at business, or organization, or staying on schedule."

He looked down, fighting for the right words. He didn't want their last few months together to be contentious. When he looked back up, her gaze connected with his. "You are the most, the *only*, practical designer I know. You're unique, Lily. You're creative, but you also understand that making a pair of two-thousand-dollar shoes might impress a fashion magazine but isn't going to translate well to the general public."

"That actress you used to work for paid three grand for a pair of pumps once."

"When she was off her meds she'd buy a plastic grocery bag for three thousand dollars." Diva didn't even begin to describe that disastrous woman. "And I don't count Hollywood people as the general public. You creating a line for Target is what I'm talking about."

"But you—"

"*Your* idea. I just typed some contracts and used big words to impress their lawyers."

She shrugged, but he knew his reminder had helped. He rose and refilled her glass, then pulled her to her feet. "This is a party, right?"

She circled her finger in the air. "Whoopee."

He tapped his glass against hers. A down-in-the-dumps Lily frankly scared him almost as much as a quiet one. "Tell me about the rhinestone sandals you were working on earlier. Glitter always cheers you up."

5

"IT'S TIME to stop playing Little Miss Nice," Lily announced over the thumping club music later that night.

Kristin and Gwen raised their martini glasses. "We salute the diva."

"It's time to get serious."

"And nasty," Gwen added.

Lily set her jaw and narrowed her eyes. "Down and dirty, if necessary."

"Cheat," Kristin said.

"Lie," Gwen added.

Lily stared at them. They all exchanged surprised looks, then burst into laughter. "I don't need to lower myself that far."

Kristin waved her hand. "Of course not."

"No one's worth your integrity," Gwen agreed.

Lily sipped her pomegranate martini, which matched her hot-pink satin halter top. Since her disastrous caviar break earlier in the day, she'd rediscovered her determination. She hadn't moved James at all on this awful retirement thing, so she'd taken a couple of positive, just-in-case steps to remind herself she had managed to run her business before he arrived, though not very efficiently.

She'd called her accountant—who basically just

did the company taxes and advised James occasionally—and asked him about her financial security, her growing profits and investments. He promised to draw up a report and send it next week.

She also called the production manager at the warehouse where her shoes were assembled and stored to find out about inventory and whether orders were being fulfilled on a timely basis. Everything was on schedule and costs were being balanced with labor and materials efficiently. Naturally, James had everything running like a dream, and she'd swallowed her fear that she wouldn't be as good.

After that businesswoman explosion, she'd needed a martini, but she felt more in control and ready to change the battleground regarding James.

"So, where do I attack next?" Lily asked her buddies.

"The girlfriend's the weak point," Gwen said.

Kristin nodded. "I agree. All that crap about puppies and women. Pu-leeze. Hip and available chicks do *not* wander about in Connecticut."

"Hi, Gwen."

They all looked up to see Ricky Desmond standing next to their table, practically drooling on Gwen.

Lily suppressed a groan. She did *not* have time for this.

Gwen leaned back as far as possible from Ricky and smiled wanly. "Hi."

Ricky was a fellow computer geek—though Gwen would smack her for using that word as a description—in Gwen's office building. He'd been chasing her shamelessly for years. And Gwen was either too kind to break his poor, nerdy heart, or she secretly liked having an admirer. Most men were intimidated by her, so Lily gave Ricky points just for sheer nerve.

But not tonight.

"You wanna dance?" Ricky asked in his nasally voice that made him sound as if he had a perpetual cold.

"Not right now. I'm here with my friends. You remember Kristin and Lily, don't you?"

Ricky smiled, exposing the gap between his teeth. "Oh, yeah. I bought my mom a pair of Lily's shoes for her birthday."

Sales. *That* was a subject Lily could warm up to. "Really? Did you see the new display at Bloomingdale's? They did such a nice—"

"I bought them in Chinatown. This guy on the corner gave me a great deal."

"China—" Horrified, she stopped. "Those are knockoffs!" She jumped to her feet, grabbing Ricky by his polka-dotted bow tie. "Where? What corner?"

Gwen stood, pulling her away from Ricky. "Lily, please. It's one pair."

Lily flounced back in her chair. After the last few difficult days, this was not the kind of news she needed. James kept that kind of stuff under control. One pair would turn into ten thousand once he left. The new self-reliance she'd found in her business skills faltered.

"You should probably go, Ricky," Gwen said.

Reluctantly, Ricky shuffled off.

When Gwen resumed her seat, Lily glared at her. "I'll remember that crack about one pair when I make copies of one of your programs and sell them on the corner of Thirty-fourth and Lexington."

Gwen raised her well-groomed eyebrows. "And how exactly will you make those copies without me to show you how?"

Kristin patted Lily's arm. "Don't pick on her. It was a good move for getting rid of Ricky."

"Sorry," Gwen said. "It *was* a good move. And I'll find out tomorrow where he got the shoes. Okay?"

Lily felt a bit better, but her party mood was rapidly going down the drain. "Okay."

"We were talking about the availability of women in Connecticut," Kristin said.

"But James's—" Lily couldn't bring herself to say *girlfriend* for some reason. "The woman he's dating is a schoolteacher. Wouldn't Connecticut be a thigh-melting place to work?"

"Probably," Kristin said. "That's why you have to keep them apart. You said they haven't been seeing each other long. Absence, as all women know, does *not* make the heart grow fonder."

Gwen leaned forward. "You've got this fashion show coming up, so there's plenty of work to be done, right?"

Intrigued by this plan, Lily nodded. "Right."

"Pile it on James," Gwen said. "Show no mercy."

"I've just spent the last week falling all over the man to please him!"

Kristin waved her hand in dismissal. "He's probably used to you changing your mind every few seconds."

Lily glared at Kristin. "I do *not* change my mind every few seconds."

"Ladies," Gwen interrupted. "Focus. Give James extra projects, have him follow up on everything you can think of."

Kristin pursed her lips. "And have him answer the phone while you're at it. That flighty Garnet barely knows which end of the receiver to talk into."

"She's getting better," Lily said. "You should have seen us yesterday, Gwen. Normal as a pair of bankers."

Gwen drained her glass. "That gives me a really weird mental picture."

"I'm not so sure that whole normal-day thing was a good idea anyway," Kristin said. "The pedicures went over much better, didn't they, Lily?"

Lily wasn't so sure about that. James had been *extremely* reluctant. "Well…"

Gwen laughed. "I just don't see Mr. Stick-In-The-Mud James getting nail treatments."

Though Lily had often thought the same thing, her emotions seemed more on edge tonight, and the idea of anybody putting down James annoyed her. The stress of possibly losing him must be getting to her. "James is not a-stick-in-the-mud. He's just conservative."

Her friends exchanged a look. "Are you sure you don't have the hots for him?" they asked together.

"Of course not. Cut it out. I need you two to help me think."

"Okay," Kristin said. "Can you find stuff for him to do?"

Lily shrugged. He was already doing so much. The other designers had dumped the set building on him, in addition to all the other projects he had going on. "I guess. I could put him on to the counterfeiting problem. He usually does things without me asking, though."

"So make stuff up," Gwen said.

"Make stuff up?"

"Yeah." Gwen signaled the waitress for another round. "Like when he's just about to leave the office, you can ask him some complicated question."

"Like what? Ask him to explain the federal budget system?"

Gwen rolled her eyes.

"I see what she means," Kristin said. "And actually, the financial angle is good. But ask him to explain some kind of *personal* financial thing. The status of your stocks or bonds or whatever."

"And after my eyes glaze over?"

Gwen accepted the fresh drinks from the harried-looking waitress, then passed them around.

The bass-laden music continued to beat in the background, and Lily rubbed her temples. Maybe this wasn't the best place to strike such an important plan. And she wasn't sure she was crazy about the plan, anyway. It seemed sneaky, a bit dishonest, like...lying.

"You do know something about your finances, don't you?" Gwen asked when they all had their drinks.

This time Lily rolled her eyes. "Of course I do. I just don't dwell on it. That's what I have James and my accountant for."

Kristin grinned and lifted her glass in a toast. "She needs to keep her mind free to *create*."

Lily poked her with her elbow.

Kristin rubbed her arm. "Hey, I wasn't making fun. It's a good strategy *and* the main reason we need to make sure James is around to do all his business-management magic."

"*And,*" Gwen added, "in the meantime, you should learn details about your financial status. If James does leave, it could be a while before you'd trust someone new to give you advice."

"I did that already. I'm fine."

But for how much longer?

BOLD WITH HER SECOND martini, Lily rode home in a cab, determined to begin the "Pile on the Work" campaign. And if she felt a pang of guilt for causing trouble in James's personal life—which she had no right to interfere in—she reminded herself how miserable a born New Yorker was bound to be in the country. He just didn't know it yet.

As she opened the door, she decided she'd take a long, hot bath in the Jacuzzi and plan her strategy for tomorrow. But as she walked down the hall toward the door connecting her apartment to the office, she noticed light streaming from James's open office door.

A glance at her watch confirmed it was nearly eleven. The pang of guilt turned into a full-fledged attack. She hadn't even kicked off the campaign yet, and already he was working until all hours. How could she ask more? How could she—

She stopped as she reached the door. His chair was empty.

Laying one hand over her racing heart, she felt along the wall, intending to turn off the switch he'd obviously forgotten. Then she noticed him, sleeping on the couch at the far end of his office. A file folder lay across his stomach. One arm dangled over the side, his knuckles brushing the sage-green carpeting.

A whole different kind of pang thumped through her body.

He was so peaceful looking. So boyish, handsome and…sexy. She took several steps toward him almost before she realized she'd moved. He'd removed his tie and unfastened the first few buttons of his white dress shirt. Dark hairs peeked from between the folds. His normally focused gray eyes were hidden behind closed lids.

Lily paused beside the sofa, gazing down at him as her heart kicked up speed. She'd never seen him like this—reclined, unaware…vulnerable. Had she really piled so much on him that he was exhausted enough to fall asleep at work?

Then she realized she probably shouldn't be there, staring at him. She was clearly invading his privacy. Considering she was also secretly plotting against him, she figured she'd pushed her conscience just a bit too far. She turned to go.

He stirred, mumbling, "Lily."

She stopped, whirling. Had he said her name?

Moving closer, sure she'd imagined his words— "Lily."

She clamped her hand over her mouth to keep a squeal from escaping. That did not sound like an I'm-sick-of-Lily-and-ready-to-dump-her-and-retire sigh. *In fact…*

Head angled, she leaned over him. That sigh sounded distinctly…erotic.

Oh, now you've really lost your mind, Lily. The man is not having erotic fantasies about you in his sleep.

But she found herself fascinated by his chest, moving up and down in time to his breathing. The bare slice of skin exposed by his open shirt begged—

Might cause him to catch a cold, then come down with pneumonia.

Right. She was *concerned*. She didn't actually feel…desire for her assistant. Not possible. Not appropriate—even for her.

What she needed to do was wake him up. The poor man wouldn't be able to sit straight for the next three days if he spent the whole night on that couch.

Plus, there was that lurking pneumonia danger.

Feeling distinctly odd at being alone with him when he was rumpled and sex— And in danger of a life-threatening illness, she dropped to her knees beside the sofa. His body heat was the first thing that assaulted her senses. She fanned her hand in front of her face. She could no doubt turn off the furnace and still be perfectly comfortable.

He also smelled wonderful. Spicy and masculine. Not overpowering.

Lily closed her eyes and inhaled deeply.

Stop, you goofball. Just nudge the man's shoulder and get out.

She poked his shoulder with one finger.

He didn't move.

But his bare chest looked really—

She nudged his shoulder with more force, but he just shifted his leg.

Planting her hands on her hips, she glared down at him and considered shouting, "Fire!" But then it was most likely her fault he was in this exhausted condition in the first place. The "Pile on the Work" campaign was looking more unethical by the moment.

Her conscience was really such a pain in the ass sometimes.

But his chest really was—

She leaned over him, ready to shake him with both hands, when his eyes flew open.

Jolted, she lost her balance and braced her hand against his bare chest.

They stared at each other for several long moments. Then they leaped apart as if the other had just caught fire.

Lily darted across the room, smoothing her hair and clothes as she moved.

James jumped to his feet. The folder and its contents spilled onto the floor. He buttoned his shirt and straightened his tie as he talked to himself. "I was, uh...sleeping—uh...dreaming." He raked his hand through his hair, so several clumps stood out at angles. "I didn't know what I was doing." He stopped, frowning. "What did I do?"

"Nothing. Absolutely nothing."

He waved his hand toward her. "What were you—"

"Nothing!" She backed toward the door. "I just, uh—" Her gaze latched on to the folder. She pointed at it. "I was going to, uh, move the folder, then wake you up, but then you, uh...you woke up."

He picked up the folder. "I was reading over the cost projections for the Spectacular."

Lily stared at this man she'd worked with every single day for the last nine months and realized...

"Your hair is sticking out all over."

He tucked the folder beneath his arm and smoothed his hair. "I was sleeping," he said.

She nodded. "Right. I was...leaving."

"Then how did you get..." He gestured toward the sofa.

"I don't know!" She thrust her hands on her hips. "I saw the light. I came in to check on you, then you were...there." She pointed at the sofa. "You said my name."

James froze. "I what?"

"In your sleep you said my name."

"It was a mistake." He looked wildly around, as if any excuse for why he'd erotically mumbled her name in his sleep would jump up and grab him. "I must have been thinking about something important I needed to tell you. You know, tomorrow. At work."

That actually made sense, and she was apparently still under some kind of odd spell, because that disappointed her. "Right."

He walked toward her, then retreated. "How about we forget the whole thing? You'll go out. I'll stay here." He paused, looking around. "Actually, I'll go down to my apartment. You go to yours. We'll come to work tomorrow like none of this ever happened. What did happen again?"

"Nothing."

A shaky laugh escaped him. "Of course. Nothing."

Lily stared at him. She remembered the warmth of his skin, the hard planes of his chest, the desire that had sneaked through her body.

And realized she'd wanted him. Still wanted him.

No. No, she didn't. She wanted James as her assistant, not her lover. In fact, anything personal between them was completely impossible. They weren't compatible in the least. She needed to keep him here to organize her office. That was her goal. That was it.

"None of this ever happened," she said, then turned and raced from the room.

She had a plan. A good plan.

And no distractions were allowed.

AT LEAST HE WASN'T having erotic fantasies about Lily in his sleep.

Though James had had a weird dream about her wearing a dark gray suit and her hair in a bun as she whacked his knuckles with a ruler.

No wonder he was falling asleep on the job. In addition to not sleeping over the guilt from leaving her and retiring, he was obsessing entirely too much over her wardrobe.

Between that and his parents' summons to referee their latest fight this morning, he had a raging headache.

He dropped his head against the cab's window, still confused by last night's name-mumbling. What was that all about? Stress? Guilt? At least he hadn't said, "Please stop hitting my knuckles with that ruler."

Still, he couldn't forget the oddly soft look in her eyes. He'd just woken up, so maybe he'd imagined that. There wasn't anything personal between him and Lily, after all. Strictly against his office policy, no matter how beautiful the woman.

One time in his career he'd gone to a personal level with a client, and he'd promised himself he wouldn't let it ever happen again.

He'd been an assistant to a successful model, and he'd grown tired of her constant disrespect for his time and efforts, so he'd resigned. She'd tried to seduce him back. And he'd let her—for about five minutes. Thankfully, he'd come to his senses short of completely selling out his integrity.

But hadn't the situation with Lily last night come about in an entirely different way? There hadn't been a conscious effort by either one of them to—

Do nothing. *Absolutely nothing.*

Well, she *had* touched him. He rubbed his chest where it felt as if her small, soft hand was still branding his skin. Not that it meant anything. Just an accident. No big deal.

His cell phone rang as the cab pulled up to his parents' building.

"Where are you?" his mother asked when he answered.

"Right outside. I'll be up in a minute."

"Hurry. Your father is threatening to throw me out the window."

Oh, this one was going to be a doozy, all right. "Hang on to his golf trophy," he advised before he disconnected.

He paid the cabbie, then buzzed his parents' apartment.

"Come on up, James, darling," his mother called cheerfully.

That was his mother's subtle way of trying to get him on her side before the presentation-of-evidence portion of the trial. Kind of like bribing the jury. Not exactly ethical, but usually effective.

He trudged into the elevator, then rode up to the eleventh floor, hoping, but not really believing, he could find a quick resolution to the conflict.

All hope was dashed the moment James walked into the apartment. His mother stood on one side of the room, his father on the other. Yellow police tape—no doubt lifted from the set of their current off-Broadway play, *The Murder of the Bald Man*—stretched down the center, cutting the sofa, coffee table, TV and kitchen area in half. His parents glared at each other over the two-inch-wide neutral zone, his father's favorite golf trophy tucked beneath his mother's arm.

"Good morning," he said, crossing to kiss his mother's cheek.

She took her gaze off her adversary long enough to look at him from head to toe. "You look tired, darling. Not sleeping well?"

"I'm fine, Mother." He turned to his dad, giving him a quick hug. "You don't look homicidal to me."

He raised his silver eyebrows. "Your mother exaggerated—as usual."

His mother brandished the trophy. "Insult me, will you, you old coot—"

Snagging the trophy and setting it aside, James smoothly stepped between them. "Why don't you state your case first, Mother. With*out* insults or threats, please."

She pushed her frosted-blond hair behind her ears, drew herself up to her full height of five foot three, did some deep breathing, then rolled her shoulders. James braced himself for the impassioned speech that was sure to follow all this preparation.

"*He,*" Fedora began, pointing at her husband, "thinks your retirement is a good idea."

Feeling a stab of guilt for being part of the cause,

he waited for the rest of it. And waited. And waited some more. "That's it? He likes the idea of me retiring, and you—what? I guess you don't."

"That's it," his father put in. "Told you she exaggerated."

His mother glared at him. "I needed his support to talk you out of this crazy idea of leaving the city. And he—he told me to…butt out!"

James glanced from one to the other. "So you're fighting about *me*?"

"Not you, darling. Your retirement. This move to Connecticut." She wrinkled her delicate nose. "All they have there is chowder."

He should have known his flamboyant, urban-loving mother would side with Lily. And be just as stubborn. "We talked about this last week, Mother. I thought you understood why I need to retire."

She sighed dramatically. "I tried to, I really did. And a café sounds charming. But I just can't bear the thought of you being so far away."

His father shook his head. "He's not moving across the country, Fedora."

She laid her hand over her eyes. "Don't remind me about those awful years he was in L.A."

"He'll be a couple of hours by train," his father went on.

"How will he come to performances? How can we meet for dinner? What if I have one of my panic attacks?"

Remorse pulsing through his body, James clutched her hands. "We can still do all those things."

"What about Lily? How can you leave her? You know how she relies on you."

"Lily will be fine. I'll help her find somebody else."

"You can't go, James," she said, her eyes watery and pleading. "You just can't."

"Fedora, please. Let the boy run his own life."

"I'm not talking to you." To prove it, she turned her head.

Meeting James's gaze, his father held up his hands, as if saying *see what I have to work with?*

James squeezed his mother's hands, then walked across the room, dropping onto the sofa.

"You're on his side!" his mother yelled. "I knew you'd take his side. And after all I've done for you. I'm your mother! How could you—"

"Mother, *please.*"

She continued to stare at him with betrayed, tear-filled eyes.

The woman was a hell of an actress. Those three Tonys hadn't been a fluke.

Still, he slid to the center of the sofa and under the yellow crime-scene tape, which rested down the center of his head. "Better?" he asked.

Her lower lip trembled. "Much."

He loved his parents, but this was just the kind of scene he was hoping to avoid when he'd moved. He'd envisioned them not calling him for every little argument and the I'm-really-going-to-divorce-him-this-time hysterics.

But he hadn't counted on his mother's stark disapproval of his retirement. When he'd told her, she'd frowned, told him he'd change his mind, then rushed off for a costume fitting. Maybe he had cheated a bit by telling her the day before opening night, knowing she'd be distracted and excited about her performance.

She was so gracious and sensitive of other people's feelings. He knew she'd worked hard to pass those qualities on to her only child—even if he was male. He owed her his understanding and patience. But did he owe her his life?

How many times had he refereed their arguments and breakups, only to have them stare at each other in a way that it seemed the whole world fell away and only the two of them, and their passion for each other, existed?

He needed some distance.

He also had a million things to do at the office, so he rose and kissed his mother's cheek. "I've got to go to work, Mother."

Her mouth dropped open. "You—*what?*"

"Bye, Dad. I'll be at the office if you need me."

Smiling, his dad waved. "Bye, son."

"James!" his mother cried when he reached the door. "We've drawn a line down the center of our apartment. I'm in tears. You *have* to help us."

Over his shoulder, he gave her a wan smile. "I came. I understand. I hope things work out."

She started toward him. "But you're still not going to retire, are you? I need you here."

"Yes, I am." Before she could do more than gasp, he opened the door and stepped out. "I'll see you later in the week. We'll have dinner."

He might regret cutting off his mother later, but right now he was just too tired to argue. He'd changed his plans, abandoned his ambitions for culinary school or earning a business degree a long time ago to help his family.

He'd achieved a certain level of success in his life.

He'd worked hard and saved well. He'd done every-thing they'd ever asked of him. He was going to leave his job and move to the country.

And neither tears. Nor guilt. Nor pleading eyes were going to stop him.

MAYBE SHE SHOULD GIVE HIM the pleading, tearful eyes. *Nah.*

She was low, but not that low. Besides, it hadn't worked the other day in the conference room—even accompanied by champagne and caviar. No, it was best she keep her distance from her assistant. Last night had been a step in a direction she hadn't expected.

Not that her view of him had changed at all—even with a glimpse of that fabulous chest of his. She liked him as an anally organized business manager. But as a man? *Nah.* Last night was just a hormonal-overflowing thing.

Still, she'd avoided him and his office all morning. She didn't want to go in there and be tempted to think about that moment she'd leaned over him, the way his hard chest had felt beneath her fingers. Bad idea. Better to stay focused on keeping him busy and keeping her business solvent.

Shaking aside the trouble with James, Lily concen-trated on the one thing that had always kept her on track and motivated—her work.

She smiled as she put the finishing touches on a design for an orange-and-white sandal with a row of daisies covering the strap across the toes. Her collec-tion for the Spring Spectacular was something to be proud of. The designers involved had given her a bit of direction in the focus of their styles. Some wanted casual, some professional, some glitzy, but they'd just sent her the sketches for the clothes and pretty much left her to produce her own ideas.

The designer with the orange collection was nearly done and ready to go, and later in the week she had a meeting with the other two designers to show them the last few pairings of shoes and outfits. Then, once the runway backdrop was completed, only the rehearsals and the show itself were left to tackle.

The show that might well be her last with James.

"Lily?" Garnet called from the doorway of the workroom.

Lily continued to stare at her sketch pad. "Yeah?"

"You should let me go tonight."

"No."

"I could wear one of the new designs." She leaned around Lily. "It could be great publicity."

Lily waved her hand as if shooing a fly. "Go away, Garnet. I'm working."

Garnet, as usual, ignored her request. "I could be a great contact for you, you know. I have lots of friends with lots of money."

With a sigh, Lily finally set down her pencil. She crossed her arms over her chest and glared at her receptionist. "We tried that. Your friends came to my fashion show—which cost me thousands in model fees and refreshments, by the way. They ate and drank and watched. Then drank some more. Then decided to go partying and not purchasing." She shook her head. "Pardon me if I'm a little reluctant to go down that road again."

Garnet smacked her gum and rolled her eyes. "That was *three whole months* ago. I have new friends now."

Lily had a fund-raiser for a charity that night, and had been so concerned Garnet might run off with the shoes she was donating for the auction that she'd locked them in the safe. Inviting Garnet to go to the fund-raiser, representing Lily Reaves Shoes, wasn't going to happen.

Still, she felt bad for the girl, who'd been spoiled by her father, ignored by her mother, and fickle with her friends and lovers. She seemed to have no direction in her life. Lily had hoped this job would at least give her some business experience. Though she *had* shown interest in design on "normal" day. Maybe she, like Lily, just didn't gel with the regular business world.

She shook her head. "You can't wear the shoes, Garnet, but sometime in the next couple of days we'll work on designing a pair for you."

Garnet clapped her hands. "Really? That would be so cool."

"Any chance for a repeat performance of normal day?"

Frowning, Garnet smacked her gum. "Do I get another pair of shoes?"

"Garnet," James said as he walked into the room. "I need you to take these papers to Fabian LaRoche's office." As he handed a folder to the receptionist, his gaze darted to Lily. "Morning," he said, then returned his attention to Garnet before she could even nod. "He needs to sign the papers and have his secretary notarize them. You'll need to sign as a witness."

Garnet tucked the folder beneath her arm and started for the door. "Yeah. All right."

James's serious gaze pinned her in place. "Don't shop on the way there or back. Don't stop for coffee at Starbucks. Don't stop for a quick facial, hair appointment, nail repair or foot massage. I need you back here to catch up on some filing."

Garnet huffed in frustration, but obviously decided James wasn't in the mood for more of a protest than that. "I'll be good." She swished out of the room.

As the sound of her footsteps faded away, Lily focused her attention on her drawings. The silence between her and James didn't feel like the companionable quiet they'd shared during the workday so many times in the past. The air felt thick with tension. Her stomach tightened.

James cleared his throat. "How are the drawings coming?"

"Fine."

"You'll be ready for the meeting?"

"Yes."

"Great." He walked to the door, but before he crossed the threshold, he stopped. "Is it going to be like this from now on?"

As if she had no idea what he meant, Lily continued to stare at her drawing. "Like what?"

"Silence. Short answers. Unable to look at each other."

She should have known James wouldn't just leave last night alone. If they ignored that moment when they'd stared at each other as if they…*wanted* each other, wouldn't it just fade away? "I'm fine, aren't you fine?"

"I think we should talk about it."

"I don't."

"Lily, we need to—"

She slammed her pencil on the drafting table and

rose. "I don't. For one thing nothing happened. We just—it was just an awkward moment." She stalked toward him. "We're both under a lot of stress. The Spectacular, your—" She couldn't bring herself to say *retirement*, so she settled for "—announcement."

Relief slid through his eyes. "Right. The stress. I just—" His face flushed. "I didn't say anything inappropriate, right?"

She shook her head. "No." *Though you did sigh kind of erotically, just after you said my name...*

"Because you know how much I value my professionalism around the office."

"Of course."

"I'm glad we're comfortable with each other, and we're friends, right?"

"Oh, yeah."

"But we also have to work together, and that requires a certain amount of distance, doesn't it?"

That all sounded so good, and so...false. He might believe in the propriety of what he was saying, but she couldn't get the sight of a sliver of his bare chest out of her mind. "Of—" She stopped, locking gazes with him. Her stomach bottomed out. Oh, hell, it was happening again. "Of course." She took several steps back.

He rolled his shoulders. Shoulders she'd shaken, touched and longed to caress. "Great. So we're all right again?"

"You bet."

LILY SMOOTHED her lavender cocktail dress and checked her reflection in the full-length mirror. Fabian did know how to make the best of any woman's figure. The slim lines of the dress hugged her waist and hips but didn't cling or overemphasize any one area of her body.

And she definitely appreciated his special rates for the Spectacular shoe designer.

This was exactly what she needed—a night out. People, laughter, champagne, a beautiful dress, new shoes. She could distance herself from thoughts of James leaving, or worse, of him staying and her continuing to think about him and…want him.

"You don't want him," she said to her reflection.

She needed James's business expertise, not his body. It was time to get a hold on her libido and get back to her plan of keeping James busy, to show him how indispensable he was to her business. She'd never let a man distract her from her career goals before, and she certainly didn't intend to start now.

She snagged her metallic lavender shoes from the closet and had just buckled one, when the phone rang. Hobbling to the bedside table, she hit the speakerphone button. "Hello?"

"Where are you?" Gwen asked.

"On my way. Worked too late."

"You're supposed to be dumping work on James, not taking on more yourself," Gwen reminded her.

"I know. I'm going—" She stopped as the doorbell rang. "God, what *now?* I gotta go, Gwen."

Lily disconnected and, still holding her other shoe, hopped to the door. She hesitated before grasping the knob. The last time James had knocked on her apartment door he'd told her he was leaving. She really wasn't sure she wanted to know what awaited her this time.

Maybe she could sneak out the other door. Turning, she tiptoed away.

Bang, bang, bang. "I know you're there, Lily," James said.

Damn, damn, damn. She stopped, glaring over her shoulder at the closed door.

"I heard you talking," he continued. "This is important. Open up."

She stomped back to the door, then flung it open. "What?"

He looked tired and irritated. "Come in, James. Have a seat, James. Want a glass of wine, James?"

Dream on, buster. She wasn't in the mood for graciousness. She stepped aside so he could enter. "Park yourself on the sofa. You've got two minutes."

But he didn't cross the room and sit on the sofa. He crossed the room and *dropped* onto the sofa. "Carlotta Gambini called."

By the look on his face, they obviously hadn't discussed what a great job they were all doing. "What's wrong?"

"Orange is out. Pink is in."

"Pink what?"

James massaged his forehead with his fingers. "Clothes, shoes, everything. She wants everything pink."

"Are you telling me that the designer, who just a month ago told me that orange was this season's absolutely-can't-do-without color, and therefore designed her entire collection around that color, has now *changed her mind?*"

"Yep."

She snapped her fingers. "Just like that?"

"Looks like."

"We've already made nearly a dozen pairs of shoes."

"I realize that."

"The show is just over three weeks away."

"I realize that, too."

She sank onto the sofa beside him. "We'll never make it in time."

"Yes, we will." He straightened, rolling his shoulders. "I'll call the factory and have them stop production immediately. I'll talk to the fabric and leather people first thing in the morning for new samples." He rose, his face set with determination. "Oh, and I'll call Teresa."

Lily looked up at him. "Teresa?"

"To cancel our date." He strode across the room, heading toward the office. "Go on to your party. Don't worry about things here. You can start fresh on new designs in the morning."

Lily swallowed. This was just the sort of situation James thrived in. He kept calm, he outlined a plan and he made things happen. *Don't worry about things here.*

In addition to him handling the crisis, her plan was under way without her making a single move. She was getting just what she wanted. James was working at all hours. He was about to cancel a date. And she was going to a glitzy party.

It was perfect.

So why did it feel so wrong?

James had just opened the door when Lily called to him. Stop."

Looking confused, he glanced over his shoulder. "Stop what?"

With one shoe on and one off, she hobbled toward him. "Stop working." She took a deep breath, then let it out. She bit her lip. Swallowed. Muttered to herself.

He looked as if he wanted to strangle her. *"What?"*

"Go on your date. I'll stay here and get started on the new designs."

He angled his head. "You want me to— *What?*"

She shoved him through the doorway. "Go. Go now. Quick. Before my selfish genes come back and take over."

Turning, he shook his head, and she couldn't help but sigh at how dedicated he was to her. He really was the best.

"We're in this together," he said. "I'm staying."

"No." She couldn't let him do it. This was *her* business, and it was time she stopped dumping on him. She would have to find another way to change his mind about leaving. "You can't talk to anyone at the production warehouse or the suppliers tonight. But the designs need to be tackled immediately. I need to work. You go play."

James stared directly into her eyes. "Who are you, and what have you done with Lily Reaves?"

"Continue to make fun of me and I'll put superglue on your computer keyboard while you're gone."

"I'm still retiring."

She turned away, pulling off her shoe. "Yeah, yeah, yeah." That was a problem for another day. With the straps hanging from her fingertips, she walked down the hall toward her workroom.

"Aren't you going to change first?"

"No. I'm going to dance with myself and drink wine, and I want to look good while I do it."

6

YOU DON'T HAVE any problem looking good.

As James watched Lily saunter down the hall, the thought popped unbidden into his mind.

He looked away to prove to himself he had self-control when it came to those eye-popping legs of hers. And, before he could let his cynical side question her motives for this selfless gift, he grabbed his jacket from his office, then headed out. Checking his watch, he realized that even if he was halfway there, he'd still be a good fifteen minutes late.

He called Teresa on her cell and told her he was on his way, but as he climbed into a cab, his thoughts were on Lily. She was up to something. Again. Actually, the same thing, just a different angle, if he wanted to get technical, which he really didn't—

He cut himself off. He couldn't even think straight when he was *thinking* about her these days.

It wasn't right. Or professional. And certainly not productive. Still, an image of her in that silky, sparkly dress invaded his thoughts. His memory provided a clear, full-length picture of her, starting at the top of her head, with her dark hair partially pulled up and the rest of the wavy strands brushing her shoulders. Her pale skin glowed, highlighted by the delicate amethyst necklace around her throat. The pale purple of the dress complemented her eyes and coloring perfectly, and he envisioned sliding his hand across her bare—

"Hey, pal, we're here."

James shook himself from his fantasy and paid the cabdriver. He rolled his shoulders as he headed across the sidewalk toward the sports bar where he was supposed to meet Teresa. He shouldn't be thinking about one woman on the way to meet another.

Teresa was the woman he was dating. She was the one he should be thinking about touching. She was the one he should be saving mental images of. His quest for a new life did not include Lily, or any part of her wild and unpredictable world. Teresa fit into his plans.

Still sitting in the lobby, she greeted him with a warm smile. "Traffic?"

He kissed her cheek briefly. "Always."

Liar. And what was she doing waiting so patiently for him? Lily would never have accepted such a lame excuse. She would have at least gone to the bar and ordered herself a drink while she waited.

As the hostess led them to their table, he reminded himself that Teresa's patience was a good thing. Why would he think patience was bad? Why did he *want* her to be angry?

"You wouldn't believe what little Scotty did today," Teresa said when they were seated.

Scotty was one of the kids in her second-grade class who seemed to always be in trouble. "What?"

"Poured an entire bowl of blue paint over his head."

Talk about patience. The woman was a damn saint. "You're kidding? What did you do?"

She started into the story, and James resolutely pushed Lily from his mind. Teresa deserved his undivided attention.

All through dinner, he listened to details about her day—the silly things the kids did—in addition to the paint episode, Scotty also threw wood chips on the playground—the quiet lunch she'd shared in the teachers' lounge, the simple pleasure of watching a child's eyes light up when they learned something new.

It all sounded delightfully...boring. But good boring.

With Garnet's constant complaining and Lily trying to change his mind about leaving every two minutes, plus the sudden change of orange to pink, he felt as frustrated as if he'd been fighting through a midnight crowd at Times Square.

But part of him—a very small part—kept drifting back to Lily. Did she have a handle on what she needed to do? Did she have the supplies she needed? Could she really come up with changes on the spot, or was she stymied?

He hated not being part of the action. He enjoyed the challenge of getting things under control, of turning chaos into organized accomplishments.

He wasn't bored by Teresa's stories. No way. Not at all.

"Am I boring you?" she asked, finishing off her last French fry.

"Of course not. Handling twenty-one second-graders all day just seems like a job for an army general rather than a lovely woman."

She waggled her finger at him. "Flattery will get

you nowhere. I got the distinct impression that you were drifting."

He captured her hand and squeezed. "Impossible. You wanna go listen to some jazz?"

She shook her head. "I can't. I have an early day tomorrow. Gotta keep sharp for those kids."

"Right." But as James paid the bill, and she talked about the talent of the Yankee bullpen, he couldn't help thinking that Lily would have said, "To hell with tomorrow, let's go." A man can't have everything. No woman was perfect.

Besides, Lily wouldn't have even known what a bullpen was. And the professional thing, the *right* thing to do was to go home early, just as Teresa was doing.

Outside Teresa's apartment, he pulled her toward him for a kiss and prayed for some heat, but she just gave him a quick peck and pulled away.

No woman was perfect.

Teresa was quiet and lovely. She liked baseball and the country. She had a regular life. The heat would develop, and he didn't need reckless spontaneity. He got that all day. His mother and father had that, plus all their friends and their mates. They were all one big, constant therapy session. He didn't need drama and passion to be happy.

Still, he told the cabbie there was an extra twenty in a quick ride back to his apartment. He wanted to check on Lily before he called it a night. She would probably be deep in concentration, so he'd say little. Just a quick peek to be sure she didn't need him.

Just a glimpse of her energy and fire...

"It can't hurt to look."

"Problem?" the cabbie asked, his gruff face reflected in the rearview mirror.

"No. Just talking to myself."

The cabbie shook his head. "Picked up this chick the other night with the same problem." He paused. "Matter of fact, she was headin' to this same address."

"Knockout brunette?"

"Yep."

"That's my boss."

The cabbie raised his eyebrows. "Wanna trade jobs?"

"No, thanks."

The car rolled to a stop. "Smart guy."

James slid out—and slid the extra twenty through the window. He jogged to the elevator, then rocked on his heels as he rode up. As he unlocked the door, he wondered if they had any wine in the office fridge. She might like a glass as she worked. That was good—even sorta professional. He'd pour her a glass, then retreat to his own apartment for a beer and some ESPN. He'd pull out pictures of his farm and remind himself of the future just over the horizon and how much better his life was going to be.

He opened the door to a darkened foyer and a colorful string of cuss words.

"Damn stupid freakin' ridiculous *pink* shoe! I've had it!"

Well, she was certainly on a roll.

He walked down the hall and through the doorway without pausing. Most people might be reluctant, or at least hesitant to approach a woman in the middle of a major fit.

James rubbed his hands together.

He stopped just inside the room and simply watched Lily.

Barefoot, still dressed in her slinky lavender gown, her hair completely fallen on one side, she paced beside her drafting table. Several pairs of white shoes, in varying heel heights and styles, lay in a scattered mess on the worktable. Crumpled papers, sequins and fabric squares covered the wooden floor. A forgotten glass of wine sat on a table on the far side of the room.

She was talking to and pointing at the shoes. "I had the orange thing down. You'd think I could just switch my daisy and tangerine motif to roses and strawberries, but noooo. *You* won't cooperate! You look ridiculous. Like plastic Barbie shoes. Who's going to pay two-twenty-nine-ninety-five for *that*?"

James smiled. "Honey, I'm home."

LILY WHIRLED. What was *he* doing here? Him and his retirement crap had started this downward spiral of lousy ideas, stupid ideas, then falling all the way to *no* ideas.

Her mind was blank. Every time she closed her eyes all she saw was a giant, pink glob of cotton candy. The color wasn't bad, but the details she needed—buckles, straps, ties, patterns, decorative touches—wouldn't come.

Thanks to e-mail she had the designer's sketches and fabric designs, but they weren't sparking any thoughts.

Pumps or sandals? She had no idea. Low heels or high? She couldn't decide.

Even though she knew the root of her trouble—

Play the Lucky Hearts Game

and get...

2 FREE BOOKS
and a FREE MYSTERY GIFT...
YOURS to KEEP!

yes! I have scratched off the silver card. Please send me my *2 FREE BOOKS* and *FREE mystery GIFT*. I understand that I am under no obligation to purchase any books as explained on the back of this card.

Scratch Here!
then look below to see what your cards get you...
2 Free Books & a Free Mystery Gift!

331 HDL D345   **131 HDL D35P**

FIRST NAME

LAST NAME

ADDRESS

APT.#

CITY

STATE / PROV.

ZIP / POSTAL CODE

(H-F-12/04)

Twenty-one gets you
2 FREE BOOKS
and a *FREE MYSTERY GIFT!*

Twenty gets you
2 FREE BOOKS!

Nineteen gets you
1 FREE BOOK!

TRY AGAIN!

Offer limited to one per household and not valid to current Harlequin Flipside™ subscribers. All orders subject to approval.

The Harlequin Reader Service® — Here's how it works:

If offer card is missing write to: Harlequin Reader Service, 3010 Walden Ave., P.O. Box 1867, Buffalo NY 14240-1867

BUSINESS REPLY MAIL
FIRST-CLASS MAIL   PERMIT NO. 717-003   BUFFALO, NY

POSTAGE WILL BE PAID BY ADDRESSEE

HARLEQUIN READER SERVICE
3010 WALDEN AVE
PO BOX 1867
BUFFALO NY 14240-9952

NO POSTAGE
NECESSARY
IF MAILED
IN THE
UNITED STATES

fear, plain and simple fear of failure—she couldn't get past the block. And now James had appeared to offer a convenient target. One she wanted to hit but knew she shouldn't.

She turned back to her samples. "Go away."

He approached her, anyway—the fool. "I just came to see if you needed any help," he said calmly.

Glaring at him, she held out her arms. "Do I look like I need help?"

He raised his eyebrows. "Yes."

"Oh, yeah?"

"Yeah."

She poked him in the chest. "Well. I. Don't."

He glanced down at her finger. "I'll get you a fresh glass of wine. We'll—calmly—go over your ideas. You just need a little focus, some organization, maybe—"

"I need you to get lost." Her temper was teetering on a very shaky precipice, and he *really* didn't want to push her just now. "All the designs suck, and I can't work with you here."

"You've only been at it for a couple of hours." His tone was calm, his voice steady. "Give yourself some time. You'll make it work."

She shook her head. "I can't."

"You will. Close your eyes."

"I don't want—"

"Please." His gray eyes softened. "For me?"

Lily did as he asked, more because the probing look in his eyes made her stomach feel strange than because she wanted to please him. As the glob appeared behind her eyes, she sensed him moving closer. She could smell his cologne, feel the heat of his body.

"What do you see?"

"A giant pink glob of cotton candy."

He chuckled, and the sound pinged off her nerve endings like the little ball in a pinball machine. "Relax." He slid his hands around hers, shaking them lightly. "Let your thoughts go."

Oh, her thoughts were going, all right. Fast, on a one-way ticket to Inappropriate Land. She liked the scent of him teasing her senses. She liked the warmth of his touch. And, following his advice, she didn't halt her thoughts there, as she'd been doing all day.

She wondered about the breadth of his shoulders, the muscles on his body, the texture of his skin—all over, not just the slice of chest she'd touched the night before. Lily felt delightfully dizzy as she pictured the warmth of his smile, the calm resolve he wore as well as his tailored suits. His patience and even his uptight professionalism.

She liked his eyes and—

His eyes. Gray, clear and steady.

How would pale pink pumps with gray trim look? Maybe with small bows on the backs of the heels. Classy. Dynamite with the gray-and-pink suit the designer had sent sketches of. A way for… A way for executives to be professional, yet feminine.

Smiling, she blinked, meeting his gaze. "I've got something."

James squeezed her hands, then released them. "I knew you could do it."

Relief and adrenaline coursed through her. She wanted to shout, jump up and down, then kiss him for being her inspiration. Her gaze slid to his lips. She licked her own.

He froze, staring at her with an odd mix of surprise and curiosity in his eyes.

Her heart pounded; her palms grew damp. What would he feel like? Could their chemistry in the office change into sexual chemistry? What could it hurt to explore?

Stepping back, he headed for the door and broke the tension. "I'll get some coffee."

MORE THAN TWO HOURS LATER, Lily flopped onto the sofa. "Sorry I was such a pill earlier."

"I've seen you upset, pissed and smoke-coming-out-of-your-ears angry," James said. "But having you stare at me as if you'd like to hog-tie me and roast me over an open fire was a new one."

"Hog-tie?"

"I saw it on ESPN2 once—the Texas Rodeo Challenge."

"Ah." Now that the glow of discovery had faded, she could glance at him and smile without feeling all gushy and weird about it. Her curiosity about the sudden attraction she felt toward James was just a passing thing. Panic over his leaving. Her feminine hormones trying to show her an obvious way to get and keep his attention. "The stress is really getting to me."

Beer bottle in hand, he sat beside her. "You think?"

She glowered at him. "You started it, you know."

He sighed. "Are we going to spend the next three months arguing about this?"

"Maybe." She just couldn't admit defeat—to herself and *certainly* not to him. "You helped me earlier. Maybe I need you as my muse now." Though she wasn't about to tell him she'd gotten another inspiration by picturing herself dressed in a skimpy bit of pink lingerie, strutting toward him with seduction on her mind.

And how dare he, when he was so "ready to settle down" with Teresa the Schoolteacher, invade her thoughts and fantasies? It was completely irritating.

"You're your own muse, and let's drop it—just for tonight, please."

"Fine." He looked especially good rumpled, she decided. He'd tossed off his jacket and tie and unbuttoned his shirt partway. That slice of his chest tantalized her again.

But he was probably a lousy kisser.

Oh, yeah. He was patient, commanding *and* sensitive. A *lousy* combination.

Maybe not knowing was what was making her crazy. She should have grabbed him when she had the chance earlier.

"You made a good start on the designs tonight."

"Yeah." Now that she'd busted through the block, she wasn't nearly as worried about changing things, though she'd still like to strangle crazy Carlotta for causing so much confusion.

"I sent e-mails to the production and supply people. I drew up a new deadline schedule for you, and I'll send Garnet over to collect new samples first thing in the morning."

Frustrated by how aware she was of his proximity, Lily laid her head back against the sofa cushions. "Did Carlotta give you any reason why she suddenly decided pink was the new color?"

James shook his head. "I just talked to her assistant, who sounded pretty frazzled herself."

"Knowing Carlotta, she probably had some damn dream about a giant stick of bubble gum."

"Or her psychic adviser decided her aura had changed."

"I was having visions of cotton-candy blobs, so who am I to criticize?" She rubbed her tired eyes. "Don't suppose it matters now, anyway. We just have to deal with it."

He shrugged. "True."

As she watched him close his lips over the edge of his beer bottle, she pulled her sweatshirt away from her skin, sorry she'd decided to change earlier. "Are you hot? I think it's hot in here."

"I'm fine." He started to rise. "I could get you a beer."

She laid her hand on his arm. "No, I'm fine. Well, I'm not fine, I just—" She broke off as his gaze dropped to the spot where their bodies touched.

His gaze slid back to hers. Raw hunger glowed from his eyes.

Before Lily could remember why she shouldn't, she tugged his arm. He dropped to the sofa, and she thrust her hand in his hair, yanking his head toward hers.

At the first touch of his lips, her heart zipped to her throat, and her stomach bottomed out. She grabbed hold of the desire, thrilling in the skip of her pulse and the liquid heat flowing through her veins. Her skin caught fire as he moaned against her and his tongue swept inside her mouth. Regardless of her recent curiosity, she hadn't counted on this.

Wild need. All-consuming passion.

Was all this really hiding beneath those starched white shirts and Brooks Brothers suits? She'd expected awkwardness, a sense that she was making a mistake, but satisfaction filled her even as she hungered for more.

Then James stopped.

Oh, damn. Sensing his next move, she snagged his shirttail as he was pulling away. "Oh no you don't."

Regret filled his eyes. "We can't do this, Lily. It won't lead anywhere good."

"It was leading to a pretty damn good place if you ask me."

He rose, turning away. "I made a promise to myself. You know that."

"I'm not asking you to compromise your professional ethics. I just want your body. I say we—"

She slammed her mouth shut as he whipped his head toward her, staring at her in shock. This had gotten *way* out of hand. She'd tasted him, whetted her appetite, and she suddenly found herself starving.

She *really* needed a new diet.

"You say we...?" he prompted.

Trying like crazy to shove aside the impulse to grab him again, she shook her head. "I don't know. Nothing. I just—what's happening between us?"

"Nothing." He set his jaw, and she wasn't sure if he was trying to convince her or himself. "It's nothing."

Lily waved her hand toward the sofa. "We can't just pretend *that* didn't happen."

"Why not?"

Frankly, she couldn't come up with a single argument—logical or otherwise. But a part of her just didn't want to let go. Part of her still wondered. And wanted.

He paced for a moment, then sank to the sofa. "It's

not right. We work together. We're not compatible in the least."

She knew that. Of *course* she knew that. James wouldn't ever agree to go to a hot dance club and party till 2:00 a.m. She didn't even know if he danced at all. The waltz, maybe. He didn't like the way her friends thought her apartment and office had "open invitation" stamped on their doors. He liked quiet and solitude.

"It's not right."

She planted her hands on her hips and stared down at his bent head. "Well, thanks a lot. I'm not exactly thrilled—" She suddenly realized what he meant by right. Teresa. His girlfriend. "You're ready to move to Connecticut and settle down with Teresa." Guilt washed over her. She didn't steal other chicks' guys.

He looked up, then away. "Not exactly."

She narrowed her eyes. "What do you mean—not exactly?"

"I, uh, may have exaggerated a bit about the depth of our relationship."

"How deep would you say things are?"

"We're pretty much still wading in the baby pool."

"Well, that's just dandy." She'd actually felt guilt over not just the kiss, but plotting to break them up. Did that mean Teresa didn't stand between them? Would it really matter if she didn't? The space between her and James was already pretty full of problems.

"What have you done to me?" he asked.

"What have *I* done to *you*? You're crazy. You're the one who was sitting there looking all cute and irresistible and sexy." She clamped her hand over her mouth. She *hadn't* just admitted that.

Unexpectedly, he grinned. "Irresistible and—" Then, as if he remembered who she was—and who he was—he shook his head. "I think we've moved into a strange area here."

With her hand still over her mouth and afraid to move it in case she said anything *else* stupid and embarrassing, Lily nodded.

He stood, then backed around the sofa, across the room, and toward the office door. "I refuse to let this mess up my agenda. I have new plans for my life, a schedule to keep, and you're not on it." He walked through the door, slamming it behind him.

Lily flinched. A marriage proposal from one guy and skid marks on her lips from another. Dating in the twenty-first century was just too damn complicated.

"Hey, Lily, Carlotta Gambini wants to have dinner tomorrow night!" Garnet yelled down the hall. "Where do you want to go?"

Lily stepped out of her workroom. She glared in the general direction of the foyer and the receptionist's desk. She was absolutely *not* in the mood to deal with that girl today, but it was Friday, and she had two glorious, Garnet-free days to look forward to.

Before Lily could let loose the not-so-kindhearted thoughts running through her mind, Garnet yelled again, "Lily, did you hear me?"

Halfway down the hall, James's office door flew open. "Garnet! What the hell is going on out here?"

Lily grinned. Garnet had done it now—woken the sleeping bear. That man needed to get laid in a major way. Not that *she* was the gal to do it. He had a *schedule* to keep, and *she* wasn't on it. Not that she cared. The man would no doubt be an uptight bore in bed.

Garnet stomped into view. "I need to find out about dinner, or Ms. Gambini's assistant is going to call and yell at me—again."

James looked heavenward. "And there's a good reason why you're not using the intercom?"

"I turned it off," Lily said before Garnet could answer.

He whipped his head toward her, but he didn't meet her gaze. He deliberately stared over her shoulder. "Why?"

"I was working and didn't want to be disturbed."

His head swung back toward Garnet. "And why didn't *you* get up, walk down the hall and quietly knock on the workroom door?"

"She told me the last time I did that not to knock on her door again, or she'd strangle me with her bare hands." She pointed downward. "Plus, my toes were drying."

Lily glanced at Garnet's feet. Neon pink toe separators decorated her bare feet. Presumably, she'd spent the last several minutes painting her toenails, though Lily couldn't tell what color from this distance. At least she wasn't wearing any of the shoes for the Spectacular.

James leaned sideways, banging his head against the door frame. After a few raps, he straightened. "I'm going into my office. If anyone screams down the hall, knocks on my door or disturbs me in any way, *I'm* going to strangle them with my bare hands." He disappeared inside, slamming the door behind him.

Just as she had the night before, Lily flinched.

Today, though, she had no intention of crawling into her bed and bemoaning her unfulfilled needs and frustrations into the covers, while questioning her very sanity. No, today she was the ice queen. She was in control of her body and her emotions.

A man who kisses like James is not *uptight.*

She ignored her libido. She refused to chase him, or draw undue attention to herself. He wasn't interested in her, and she had her integrity. She also had a serious case of lust, but she could manage that. It was temporary. It *had* to be.

"Boy, is *he* in a bad mood," Garnet commented.

"He's under a lot of pressure," Lily said, turning toward the workroom.

"Uh, helllooo? The dinner? The place? The time?"

A Saturday-night work dinner—*bleacck*. Especially with the strange and flighty Carlotta Gambini. But then she didn't have to suffer alone.

"Seven-thirty. Make reservations at Angelo's." She smiled sweetly. "And make sure to send James an e-mail about the time and place. He'll need to come, too."

But as she entered the workroom, she second-guessed the idea of dinner with James. Strictly for business purposes he should be there, but she wasn't sure she wanted to be around him.

The man had spent the morning ignoring her completely. He avoided her by sending e-mails rather than popping into the workroom. He kept his door closed. The one moment they'd run into each other near the coffeepot, he'd scooted around her as if she had a communicable disease.

Oh, yes, he'd made it very clear last night who he preferred to spend time with. That blond schoolteacher.

She was probably graceful and elegant and quiet. Not high-maintenance. All the things she could never be.

Still, Lily remembered a guy she'd had a crush on in high school. She'd fantasized about him, smiled at him, helped him with his homework and waited for him to make the first move. Never happened.

She'd been a New Yorker for a decade now, and if she'd learned one thing from this city it was determination. You wanted something around here, you'd better ask for it, because nobody was worried about *your* needs. Nobody was going to ask you what *you* wanted.

If she could just figure out what she did want, she'd be much better off.

WHEN LILY APPEARED in the office foyer at precisely six forty-five the next evening, she'd made no concrete decisions. But she'd changed her mind about a few things.

For instance, the whole idea of the ice queen had fallen aside. The only way ice could be related to her was in the diamonique—aka fake diamonds, since she couldn't afford the real thing just yet—choker around her neck.

She *had* stuck by refusing to chase him. Though she'd briefly wavered a bit there, as well.

She liked him. He liked her—at least most of the time. They communicated well. They respected each other, and the talents they each brought to her business. They both liked—

Well, she wasn't really sure they both liked the same of anything. She knew he liked baseball. She understood the guys hit a ball with a bat and wore cute, tight pants. She liked going to the ballet and Broadway productions, and he…understood the guys wore cute, tight pants.

She was creative; he was decisive. She was unpredictable; he was commanding. And she could think of a million reasons why those combinations could work well in a sexual relationship.

As for Teresa, hell, she'd supposed he could continue to see her if he wanted to. She wasn't totally opposed to sharing. Besides, they were "wading in the baby pool." Obviously, James's cute way of telling her they hadn't slept together and certainly weren't on the verge of matrimony. In her book, that meant he was fair game.

But as she'd dressed, she'd decided against the chasing thing…probably because she definitely hadn't been able to hold to the last vow—drawing undue attention to herself.

She rolled her shoulders back as the door swung open and he appeared in the office foyer, muttering to himself. When he reached the edge of the receptionist's curved desk, he stopped, looking up.

His jaw dropped.

Lily couldn't help herself. She fluttered her lashes.

Maybe she shouldn't have spent the afternoon at Elizabeth Arden getting waxed, pummeled, perfumed, glossed and spray-tanned. Maybe the slim-fitting, spaghetti-strapped, satin, ending-at-midthigh, pleated minidress had been a bit much. Maybe the red patent-leather, four-inch-high, pointed-toe pumps were really over the top.

Naaahhh.

Laying her hand at her waist, she cocked her hip and smiled. "Ready to go?"

"I, uh…" He looked away, then—though it seemed reluctantly—back. "Yeah. I— What do you have on?"

She spun in a circle. "My Saturday-night party dress. Don't you like it?"

"Well…I, uh…this is a business dinner."

Gliding her hand down her sides from breast to waist, she shifted her hips back and forth. "Don't I look ready for business?"

"That depends on the business."

She walked slowly toward him. "I guess it does."

His eyes dilated. His gaze slid over her, caressing her with heat. "You look amazing."

Smiling, she studied him from head to toe—his glossy, dark hair, his tailored dark gray suit and red pocket square, then the tips of his buffed black shoes. "You clean up pretty well, yourself." She skimmed her index finger over his pocket square. "We match."

"Purely accidental. I didn't realize you'd be so…"

"Hot?"

"Well, yeah, but—"

"Stunning?"

"That too, though—"

"Sexy?"

He groaned and closed his eyes. "You're killing me, Lily."

Hmm. She'd bet her spring collection that his precious schoolteacher had never worn—

Well, hell, that was probably the point. Maybe she embarrassed him with her outrageousness. She was fine as a business associate, but as a woman, he wasn't into siren red. Another miscalculation. Another area where they'd probably never agree.

With an internal shrug and roll of her shoulders, Lily spun toward the door. The look in his eyes alone had been worth the effort. "Let's go. I'm starving."

James followed her out the door, locking it behind them. As they walked into the elevator, he said nothing, just looked pensive, maybe even nervous.

Oh, good grief. Did he think she was going to jump him in the car? "We haven't been out together in a while. It will be fun, don't you think?"

"You usually do the going out, and I stay in. Speaking of that, I'm not sure we should have accepted this invitation. I've gotten all the details about the changes from Carlotta's assistant. Do we really want to go through a dinner with her?"

She hooked her arm through his. "It's good PR. And it's fun. Did I mention that?"

He glanced sideways at her. "I'm not opposed to fun, you know."

"Really?" Personally, she wasn't betting on it.

They stepped out of the building, and Lily started toward the long, black Mercedes idling at the curb.

"You hired a limo?"

Lily smiled at the driver, who held the back door open, then spoke to her financially repressed assistant over her shoulder. "Did I mention the theme for the night is *fun?*"

After one last glance at the building behind him, James ducked inside the car. "Sometimes your definition of fun makes me nervous, Lily."

Settling back against the leather seat, she licked her lips. "I promise to be gentle."

7

JAMES SLUMPED into the sofa and plotted escape. He'd survived dinner with Carlotta, only to find himself trapped in Lily's apartment with an assortment of her never-say-enough partying friends. The whole thing reminded him of his childhood when his parents' apartment had been filled with theater people at all hours.

At dinner, he'd suffered through endless discussions of women's shoes—leathers, prints, solids, high-heeled, low-heeled and, finally, fake fur–covered, which had to be approved by Carlotta's psychic adviser. And everything was immersed in pink.

Just before he'd slipped into a coma, he'd had the strong urge to run to a pharmacy and slug down some Pepto-Bismol.

They'd left the restaurant with Carlotta in tow, who'd called Fabian LaRoche, who it seemed automatically went everywhere with at least three women. Tonight, they were all blond. They'd all converged on Lily's apartment—with its convenient open-door policy, free booze and no cover charge, leaving him wondering how he'd managed to let his life get so out of control.

And, hell, this was his *business* life. He didn't even

want to consider his personal life. The lack of sparks between him and Teresa, the wild kiss he'd shared with Lily that followed him into sleep and haunted him when he was awake.

This is ridiculous. Just get up and leave.

She wasn't holding him prisoner. He only had to take the elevator down a few flights to get to his own apartment.

The meeting was long over, and boy, would he *not* miss silly business dinners with designers when he retired. He wouldn't miss clients who consulted psychics before making professional decisions. He wouldn't miss Lily's mood swings. Or impulsiveness.

But neither could he deny that part of him craved watching her flit around the room. Part of him was drawn to her energy and fire. Part of him had enjoyed calming her down the other night and helping her through her creative block.

Would he miss the creative process when he retired? Was it possible he'd miss the spirit of the city?

As he was pondering the direction of his life, he looked up and saw her. Champagne glass in hand, she walked toward him, that eye-popping red dress hugging every curve. Her skin shimmered beneath the artful track lighting and candles placed around the room. When she reached him, she pursed her lips, painted a matching shade of red.

This is ridiculous. It's just Lily. You've seen her nearly every day for the last nine months.

She dropped next to him on the sofa. "You can go home if you're having such a miserable time."

And to think he'd started the night wondering if she intended to use that dress to seduce him into forgetting about his retirement. Not only had she done nothing of the sort—not even the slightest bit of flirting, and for Lily that was odd, since she flirted as she breathed—now she'd pretty much told him to go home and quit spoiling the fun mood of her party.

Sometimes he was such a crabby ass.

James sighed and turned toward her. "I'm sorry. I'm just tired. I haven't been sleeping well."

Her expression somewhere between neutral and I-couldn't-care-less, she sipped her champagne. "Any particular reason?"

"I think I've just spent a little too much time talking about women's shoes."

"Mmm."

His gaze, as if drawn by an invisible string, fell to her lips.

If he'd hoped she wouldn't notice his straying attention, he was dead wrong. She angled her head. "How's that schedule of yours coming?"

"Schedule?"

"The one I'm not on."

"Oh." *Why* wasn't she on it again? His gaze slid down her figure. Somewhere between a red satin dress and endlessly lovely legs, he recalled the total incompatibility of their personalities. "It's on track."

"Do you have to plan everything?"

"Yes."

Her eyes darkened, her gaze intensifying. "It's much more fun to…grab things as they come."

"You'd know."

"Oh, darling!"

James looked up to see Fabian and his blond mini-harem swooping in.

"The collection is *wonderful*," the designer said, plopping onto the sofa on the other side of Lily. "Just the thing. Those purple, patent-leather pumps…" He kissed the tips of his fingers and blew toward her. "They're primo perfect!"

Lily beamed.

Damn, she's beautiful.

James couldn't have budged his gaze from her for the world. She was like a supersize order of French fries—you knew they were bad for you, but you craved them, anyway.

"Your designs made it easy to find inspiration," she said graciously to Fabian.

"The seductress suits you as well," he said.

James coughed. The practical parts of him panicked, and the daring parts of him clapped. "The seductress?"

Lily turned her head toward him, her eyes bright with humor. "That's the name of the dress I'm wearing."

"How apt."

Even as he realized he should have called back his words, Lily grinned. This whole night wasn't working out the way he'd figured. Maybe that dress had some kind of hypnotic powers over a man.

"It's perfect for her, don't you think?" Fabian said, not seeming at all hypnotized. "I keep telling her she could have a fantastic career as a model."

Lily rolled her eyes. "Don't be ridiculous. I have too many, uh…"

"Curves," Fabian supplied.

His mini-harem—who ought to know curves when they saw them—giggled.

Fabian pursed his lips. "Now, what are the two of

you doing over here all alone?" He flicked his gaze to James. "Talking business, I bet."

For once, James couldn't plead guilty. He'd been too busy ogling his boss to actually talk about anything professional.

Fabian waved his hands toward the middle of the room, which had been turned into a dance floor by Carlotta and another designer who'd "dropped by" just to say "hi" well over forty-five minutes ago. "Go dance. Relax. Enjoy yourselves."

James met Lily's gaze. Her reluctance was obvious. He felt the same, but probably for a different reason—he was afraid to touch her.

Finally, she stood. "Come on. I'll even pick a song you like."

Maybe he should have bailed when he'd had the chance. Dancing with Lily, holding her close to his body, had mistake written all over it. But acknowledging his fear seemed silly.

She did pick a song he liked—a jazz ballad by Sarah Vaughn, and he was careful to avoid her gaze as he slid his arms around her waist. She didn't speak, just linked her hands around his neck, her temple brushing his jaw.

Closing his eyes, he let the music fill his ears, seep through his veins, and the fabric of her satin dress glide beneath his fingers. Without his I-need-to-be-professional voice invading, he could relish touching her, breathing in her scent.

The others continued to talk. Some joined them on the dance floor. But James paid little attention. He was too busy realizing he'd never felt this sizzle with Teresa. He enjoyed her company. They had the same mentality, the same outlook on life, she was the woman he *should* want, but they didn't have chemistry. Nothing like the head-spinning sensation coursing through him now had ever occurred when he was with Teresa.

There had to be a logical explanation for his sudden attraction to Lily—stress, overworking, distraction over his parents' troubles, maybe even comfort in the familiar, since he was about to embark on a new, unknown road in his life.

He reminded himself that anything other than a business relationship between them wouldn't be productive. He wanted something solid and lasting and dependable. Lily didn't fit in with his plans.

But as her breath rushed across his cheek and her sensual body warmed beneath his hands, logic dissipated. He wasn't sure if he should act on his desire or ignore it.

For the first time in his life, decision making was pulling him apart.

LILY INHALED James's masculine scent. Why did he have to smell so great, so strong and right?

She wanted to know what made that complex brain of his tick. She wanted to see him smile and laugh. She wanted to understand—even if she didn't share—his goals and ambitions. She wanted to hold him against her, to feel his body meld with hers.

Maybe she should find another man to divert her attention. James wasn't the *only* man in the city. He was just the one she wanted.

At the moment.

She reminded herself that their relationship

wasn't going to last beyond the moment. She didn't want to ruin their professional partnership just to scratch a sexual itch.

He's leaving, anyway.

Not if she could help it.

"I'm sorry I've been such a dud tonight," he said softly.

She closed her eyes against the shiver of excitement that slid down her back. "It's okay. Carlotta and Fabian can be a little overwhelming."

"Don't forget the date trio."

Lily smiled, then sighed. How could she possibly be attracted to a man who questioned—or even cared about—normalcy? She supposed growing up with dramatic Fedora had been frustrating for a person as serious as James, but lighten up already, man. "You're not going to miss any of it, are you?"

He said nothing for a moment, then admitted, "No, I don't think so."

He'd rather be in Connecticut wandering around in a *barn*? They had good music, champagne and great, colorful friends. She just didn't get why anyone would want to escape from that. "Then you're going to miss out."

When the song ended, she let him go. Carlotta stepped into the opening, and Lily deserted him with a smile. An incompatible man with great chemistry? She and her hormones needed to chat ASAP.

She wandered around the room refilling champagne glasses. As aggravating as the creative people she worked with could sometimes be, she'd never trade them for a boardroom full of suits and sour expressions. Or a barnful of chickens and cows. Been there, done that, *way* too many times.

They were all doing what they loved; they just needed to figure out a productive way to all work together. The fact that James was deserting them should have her ticked off, not have her chasing him like some kind of pitiful, desperate, talentless hack.

Maybe this retirement thing was an avenue of artistic growth for her. A test of her resolve and strength. She'd survived on her own before, and if she had to do it again...well, she just would.

A temporary retreat was definitely in order—on both a professional and personal level.

Within five minutes, James was walking behind her. "Lily, don't be mad."

She glanced at him over her shoulder and kept moving. "I'm not mad."

"I know you, and you're mad."

She poured the rest of the champagne into her own glass, then tossed the bottle in the trash. "I'm having fun. If you're not, then just go home."

He glanced toward the door. "Maybe I will. I have some reports to look over."

Looking around the room as if she was searching for someone more important to talk to, she sipped her champagne. "Sure. Go ahead."

"I hate to leave you alone."

"I doubt the party will get so out of hand that I'll have to call security."

He crossed his arms over his chest. "I'm not so sure. What man dates three women at the same time?"

"A popular one?"

"What if he decides to add you to his harem?"

Lily watched Fabian spin a woman around on either side of him as the third shimmied in front of him. "I think he's got his hands full, already."

"We could dance again, I guess."

She glanced over at him. "How could I possibly turn down such an enthusiastic invitation?"

"See, you are mad."

"That was sarcasm, sweetie, not anger."

"You think I'm dull."

"Yes."

"I'm not."

She shrugged. "If you say so."

"This just isn't my kind of party."

Lily smiled as Carlotta twirled by them, dancing with absolutely nobody but herself. "What kind of party do you like?"

"The organized kind."

"Of course. And how many organized parties have you attended?"

As if concentrating, he frowned. "You mean lately?"

"I mean *ever*."

His frown deepened. "I couldn't count them all."

"Do you have a list of the regular ones?"

"Well, there's the annual wine tasting at—"

"'Cause I'd like a copy." She paused and sipped champagne, staring at him over the rim of the glass. "I'd really hate to wander into one of those dull-fests by mistake."

"That's not funny."

"I was being completely serious."

He grabbed the champagne glass from her hand and set it aside, then he took her hand, pulling her toward the other dancers. "Come dance with me again."

Fighting back a smile, Lily let him drag her along. Was it possible he'd come to the conclusion that he belonged with her—or rather *her company*—on his own? Should she call off her schemes? That seemed like an awfully big gamble. If she closed herself off from him completely, if she accepted his decision, he might...

What? Give his notice? Shake her confidence and stability to the core?

Done already.

Ultimately, she could only be who she was. She was willing to make allowances for her employees, to make their work experience as pleasant and fulfilling as possible, but she had to be herself.

And that encompassed his role as assistant as well as this *thing* between them.

James drew her into his arms, distracting her from her thoughts. Lily slid her palms up his chest. His heart thumped beneath her hands. Her own heart beat in rapid time with his, and she bit her lip as a wave of desire washed over her.

His effect on her was as unnerving as it was intoxicating. Most of her wanted to dive headfirst into the swirl of hunger and need he invoked, but part of her wanted to run the other way from the temptation of his touch. The struggle within her was making her crazy—hence the wild fit the other night, the inability to concentrate on her work, her snappish attitude toward nearly everyone.

Probably explaining why she really wasn't much for resistance.

She let her fingers glide along the base of his hairline. His hair was silky, soft. So much about him was tough and decisive. The texture slipping through her fingers reminded her that James was much more than the face he chose to show the world most of the time. He compensated for the chaos around him by being controlled. But based on the single kiss they'd shared, she knew a wild side existed inside him. A side that was anything but dull. The very idea of touching that part of him made her dizzy with anticipation.

When Fabian bumped against her, she finally realized the CD was playing a fast song, and she and James were definitely moving to the beat of a ballad. This was what he did to her—made her surroundings disappear, her thoughts scatter.

Knock, knock, knock.

"I'll get it," Carlotta said from across the room.

That was good, because Lily didn't have any intention of moving.

"Who could that be at this hour?" James asked.

Lily shrugged. Had to be somebody the doorman knew; otherwise, he wouldn't have let them up without calling first.

"I'm sorry," said a familiar voice. "I must have the wrong apartment. I was looking for Lily Reaves."

"Oh, she's here," Carlotta said. "Come on in."

Lily glanced over James's shoulder as his mother strolled into the apartment.

She paused in the foyer, pulling her Louis Vuitton bag behind her. She looked around, seeming a little lost, and Lily rushed toward her, James on her heels.

"Mother, is everything all right?" James took her bag with one hand, and slid his other around her waist.

She shook her head, then nodded. As a single tear

rolled down her pale cheek, she grabbed Lily's hand. "I left him. I really left him this time."

Lily's throat threatened to close. She knew the Chamberlins had their arguments, but she hadn't seen anything like this coming. She should have pressed Fedora harder when they'd met for coffee a few days ago, but she'd gotten so caught up in her own drama, she hadn't checked on her friend. "Oh, Fedora, I'm so sorry."

"You left Dad?" James asked in disbelief.

"I *had* to. He— I—" She shook her head. "It's all so complicated."

Lily's gaze connected with James's. His eyes were wide with shock and worry. He obviously hadn't expected this, either.

Her heart broke for him.

Lily squeezed Fedora's hand, then turned to her guests. "Okay, family emergency, people. Party's over."

She turned off the music, and shooed everyone toward the door, while James led his mother to the sofa. Since they hadn't had a chance to eat the tiramisu they'd brought home from the dinner meeting, she sent half home with Carlotta and half with Fabian and his dates.

When the apartment was quiet again, punctuated only by Fedora's sniffles, Lily headed to the kitchen to make a pot of tea. She set the mugs and pot on the coffee table and exchanged a glance with James as she handed Fedora her mug. He seemed lost for words.

It would be up to her, she supposed. Lily took a bracing sip of tea. "Fedora, did you and Martin have a fight?"

Fedora sniffled, her gray eyes red and swollen. "He told me I was being unreasonable and stubborn."

"About?"

James rose, sliding his hand through his hair. "About me."

Lily looked up at him. "Oh."

"Mother doesn't want me to retire."

She'd suspected this reaction from Fedora, of course, but they hadn't discussed the subject. If they'd talked, would things have turned out differently? Lily didn't know, but the idea that she should have been paying more attention to her friends, rather than focusing on her own selfish needs, troubled her. *"Oh."*

"You agree with me about this, don't you, Lily? You don't want to lose him, do you? Don't you think Connecticut is a simply horrible place? Who would want to leave the city?"

Oh, boy. She definitely agreed with all that, and a dark, not-so-nice side urged her to use Fedora to get James to stay. He loved his mother, respected her opinion and needs more than any other man she'd ever known. It was one of the few areas where he reminded her of the simple fabric of life in Iowa and one of the reasons she'd initially trusted and respected his opinion.

But taking sides between mother and son, a husband and wife, was not cool. This wasn't any of her business. She'd support Fedora as a friend, but she'd have to tread a thin line between friend and her son's employer.

She rose, smoothing her dress. "I, uh—I think I'll go change and let you guys talk. This is obviously a family matter."

James gave Lily a surprised but grateful look. He grabbed the handle of Fedora's suitcase. "Come on, Mother. We'll go to my apartment and talk this through."

Fedora shook her head, her blond curls bobbing against her cheeks. "I'm staying with Lily." She paused, her eyes pleading. "As long as she'll have me."

"I—" *Oh, boy.* "I don't think—"

"Oh, please. I won't be any trouble. I need some time to think—away from my family." She directed her gaze toward her son. "Sorry, darling."

"Well, I..." Lily looked to James for support.

He inclined his head toward the kitchen. "I need to talk to you." As they rounded the bar, he said quietly, "I'm sorry about all this. I realize how unprofessional—"

"*Unprofessional?*" Lily echoed in disbelief. "Good grief, James, your mother has left your father. Now is not the time to worry about professionalism." She could hardly believe that only moments ago she was dancing with him, holding him, threading her fingers through his hair. Now a stranger stood before her. She stared up at him. "We're friends, aren't we?"

He shoved his hands in his pockets. "Yes. Of course. I just—I'm sorry she dragged you into this."

"She didn't. I'm friends with her, too. She's welcome to stay here, but I'm not getting in the middle of anything."

He paced in front of her a moment or two, then stopped, his gaze cutting to hers. "You sent everybody home when you saw she was upset."

She crossed her arms over her chest. "Did you

think I'd shove her in a corner and hope she had a good time?"

"Why didn't you join in with her complaints against my retirement and Connecticut?"

"It wasn't my place." Her heart pounded. She'd never realized his opinion of her was so low. "I guess you expected me to, though."

"I'm not sure what I expected, but I'm grateful you didn't. You were clear-thinking while I wrung my hands and felt stupid."

A slow smile teased her lips. "Well, I'll be damned. That's pretty interesting, huh?"

"It's pretty weird."

Though she'd reacted strictly on instinct, pride filled Lily. She sympathized with Fedora. She knew if she'd broken up with a guy, she sure wouldn't want a bunch of strangers to see her fall apart. But, wow, she really had accomplished something neat. She'd filled in and supported James when he needed it, instead of the other way around.

"Why don't you go home," she said, taking his arm and steering him out of the kitchen. "I'll talk to her and encourage her to get some sleep."

"Lily, you shouldn't—"

"Don't you trust me with her?" She asked the question with half hope, half challenge. No matter what the last few weeks had brought, she hoped their friendship would hold.

James nodded, holding her gaze. "I do, yes."

LILY SHUT THE DOOR behind her assistant, then turned to eye her new houseguest. It was entirely possible her quick thinking had landed her in fairly serious trouble. The man she wanted to sleep with—for reasons she *still* couldn't figure out—had trusted her to care for his sobbing, lost-looking mother. A woman who apparently shared her resistance to James's retirement. A woman who shared her love of the dramatic, her enjoyment of people, parties and laughter.

The phrase "disaster waiting to happen" blinked like a neon sign on the marquee in her mind.

Not that that had ever stopped her before.

Tentatively, she crossed to Fedora, then sat beside her. James had praised her for her quick thinking earlier, but at the moment, she had no idea how to move forward. "Would you like some more tea?"

Fedora blew her nose, her eyes watery and bleak. "No."

"Something to eat?"

"No, thanks."

How about a shot of tequila?

But since Lily herself had consumed several glasses of champagne and nobody drank tequila alone, she decided that was definitely a bad idea. Instead, she refreshed Fedora's tea and wracked her brain for the right words and tone to soothe her friend. She had no concept of marriage troubles, of course, but she wondered what she'd do if she'd just broken up with the love of her life.

Cry?

Noting Fedora's bloodshot eyes, she checked that off the list.

Hide under the covers?

That would no doubt come later tonight.

Turn to her friends for a good old-fashioned round of male bashing?

Hmm…that was something she could get into. Scream?

"That man is so impossible!" Fedora suddenly shouted.

Now we're talking, sister.

"What did he do?" she asked, at least happy they weren't awkwardly staring at each other in silence.

"He…he…disagreed with me!"

Lily liked to have her way as much as the next gal, but she also didn't have a problem with debate on any subject. Generally because—like most women—she was always right. Still she knew how the sympathetic-girlfriend-blowing-off-steam game was played. "The jerk," she said to Fedora.

Fedora stared at her wide-eyed. "He *was* a jerk. He was unreasonable and unfeeling."

Lily had met Martin Chamberlin a few times, so this assessment totally didn't fly. He seemed, in fact, to be the most patient man on the planet. One who accepted Fedora's need for drama and excitement with a smile of long understanding and deep affection.

But then maybe he was different in private. Maybe he *was* a jerk. His son certainly had *his* moments. Actually, come to think of it, all men were a pain in the ass. "Of course he's a jerk. He's a man. Did you expect understanding? Or support? Ha! It's their life's ambition to ruin your life, desert you when you need them most."

Fedora blinked as Lily rose, pacing as she got in the spirit of her indignation. "Well, uh…I guess."

"You know what you need? A girls' night out." She paused, considering her own state of mind and frustrations with men. "Hell, a girls' *week*. We'll go shopping. Clubbing. To lunch and the shows."

Fedora nodded. "Let's do it."

Lily stopped pacing and smiled. This was an agenda she could get into. And maybe it would occupy her time enough that she wouldn't constantly think about her attraction to James—or plot with his beloved mother on ways they could dirty-dog blackmail him into staying in New York. "Let's do. First thing, we've got to shop. I have lots of designer friends, and they're great about letting me buy samples and—"

"I don't have any money."

Lily lifted her eyebrows. Fedora and her husband had a very nice apartment in the city and seemed to live a comfortable lifestyle.

Fedora blushed. "I mean, I didn't bring any money with me."

"So, we'll go to the ATM and—"

"ATM?"

"You know, where you get cash."

Fedora smiled and waved her hand absently. "Oh, those cute machines where you insert a card and money comes out? My husband and James take care of that."

Lily, though she distrusted technology, fought the urge to goggle. Who didn't know how to use an ATM? "Okay, we'll go direct. Which bank do you use?"

Fedora pressed her lips together. "Hmm...I'm not sure. My husband and James take care of that."

"Uh-huh. Do you recall a symbol? A color scheme? Anything to identify the business that has control of all your financial assets?"

The importance of money was apparently lost on Fedora. "When I need money, I call James or Martin. They set everything up."

"How?"

Fedora shrugged. "I don't know. My husband and James—"

"Take care of that." Lily sank to the sofa. She had no right to judge Fedora.

This was her in twenty years. She deferred to James and her accountant for so much. She focused mainly on her designs and left the business to them. How irresponsible was that? Did she want to wind up helpless and alone, unable to even access her own money in the future? After years of struggling for every penny, had she really let things go that far?

She also hadn't realized how ingrained James was in his mother's life. Had she really been so delusional to think *she* was the sole reason for James leaving the city? She'd attributed his leaving to his job, and though she knew that had to be a factor, she accepted now that there was much more to it. Just as she had earlier, she considered him as a young, serious child growing up with Fedora.

He'd probably felt off balance and out of place. All the things Lily herself had felt with her family. They never understood why she yearned for bright lights and places to wear the elaborate gowns and shoes she'd drawn on page after page of sketchbooks.

"I'm not even sure how to go clubbing," Fedora said. "I never really dated anybody but Martin."

"I'm not talking dates. I'm talking clubbing." She sat beside Fedora. "We go out, just us girls. We dance,

have a drink or two, then go home. You can have all
the space you want."

Fedora smiled. "That sounds like heaven."

"MAN, YOU'VE LOST IT."

Annoyed already, James stared at Dalton. "You're
not helping."

"We are talkin' about *Lily Reaves* here, right?"

"Yes."

"Drop-dead gorgeous, sexy-as-hell Lily Reaves?"

"She's the only Lily I know."

"She's comin' on to you, and you're runnin' the
other way?" Dalton drained his beer. "Man, you've
lost it."

"She's not exactly coming on to me. We're sort of
coming on to each other." Realizing how idiotic and
vague that sounded, he added, "I'm staying away
from her to *keep* my sanity."

"Well, I guess you *are* staying away from her now
that your mother is living with her. Man, you've
lost it."

James shook his head. All he'd wanted was to shift
his life in a new direction. After all his hard work for
his family and everyone else, keeping their lives in
order, he wanted to do something for himself. But
ever since his announcement, his life had just spun
further out of his control. "The only time I braved
knocking on Lily's door yesterday, I found them
watching movies, crying and painting their nails."

Dalton winced. "The scent of acetone alone would
have sent me running the other way."

"Believe me, it did." He gestured with his beer
mug, indicating the sports bar they were sitting in.

"I came down here and watched basketball games." He sighed. "I can't wait to get out of this city."

"You've lost it there, too."

"I'm just tired of the whole scene. The rush, the clubs, the noise, the traffic, the drama. Straightening out everybody else's messes. Hell, you should understand, you're a lawyer."

"I'm a man, first."

Raising his eyebrows, James sipped his own beer. "But don't you ever want to retire? Slide off into oblivion?"

"Yeah. In the Bahamas, with a bodacious blond babe glistening in the sun next to me." Dalton paused. "Then, I need sex on a regular basis."

"I get sex."

"Yeah? With Teresa?"

"Well, no...not exactly. Our relationship hasn't progressed to that point."

"Can she breathe?"

"Of course."

"Then your relationship has progressed to that point."

James didn't bother to comment. He'd already spent too much time tearing himself apart about his relationship with both Lily and Teresa.

"Okay, I know. I married my high-school sweetheart, and that relationship turned out to be a nightmare. You've dated dozens of women, and now you're ready for Miss Right. But, seriously, why are you so tripped out over a relationship with Lily? The truth this time."

James gazed morosely into his half-full beer mug. She'd been so terrific the other night. Dousing the party, patting his mother's hand. The kernel of attraction toward her had burst into a full-fledged I-gotta-have-her need. "It would be all one-sided. We'd get involved, she'd get bored after a week or two, while I fell like a ton of bricks for her, then I'd spend the rest of my days wandering aimlessly and hopelessly through the dark, cold streets of New York."

Dalton said nothing for a moment, then, "You should have been a lawyer."

"Why?"

"Juries love melodramatic speeches."

"Trust me, I'm saving myself a lot of heartache later. Call it preventative measures."

"So how did you leave things with her last night?"

"I didn't get a chance to leave things anywhere. My mother was there, remember? I think we were both thrown a little off balance when I froze and she handled everything."

"I can't picture it."

"It doesn't matter." No matter how much he wanted her, he shouldn't give in to that need. In his quest for a normal life, Lily certainly wasn't part of the picture. "What am I going to do about her?"

Dalton paused with a fry halfway to his mouth. "You're really starting to scare me."

James glared at him. "Yeah?"

Dalton polished off the fry, then held up his hands. "All right. I can see you're desperate—too desperate, if you ask me. If you really want to avoid Lily—and I'm not saying that's a *good* idea—just tell her you've got plans. 'James, can you go to dinner with me and Weird Designer number four hundred twenty-three?' You say, 'Sorry, Lily, I've got plans.' Keep it simple."

"Who should I have plans with?"

"Use me if you want."

"That just might work."

"Sure it will." He paused. "And let me know if you need someone to sacrifice on the altar of Lily's libido."

James wasn't sure he really liked that plan. "Let me guess, you'll volunteer."

Dalton grinned. "Anything for you, buddy."

FOUR DAYS LATER…

James froze midstretch as Lily appeared in his office doorway.

"You and Dalton have fun last night?"

"Yeah, sure." He yawned. "Late night, though." Actually, he'd been home by ten-thirty and wouldn't have been out at all if Dalton hadn't guilted him into going to a club. But he had been up late trying to convince his dad that Fedora was fine and that she'd come to her senses any day now. He should just be patient because James had everything under control.

Yeah, right. His mother only talked to him by phone and e-mail. She was too busy shopping and "getting her life in perspective."

And seeing his dad, floundering and despondent at the love of his life leaving him, had reminded him of the dangers of romance.

"Where did you guys wind up?" Lily asked, jolting him back to the other crisis in his life.

"Green Light."

Raising her eyebrows, she crossed her arms over her chest. "Not exactly your kind of place."

Obviously, they were back to him being boring. "What's my kind of place? The opera?"

"I thought you liked jazz. Green Light is filled with hip-hop-loving kids barely out of their teens."

No freakin' kidding. He didn't know how Dalton kept up. He'd downed three Tylenol when he came home to get rid of the pounding behind his eyes. "Great place," he managed to lie.

"I thought so."

"Certainly popular. I—" Her words finally sunk in. "*You* thought so?"

She settled her lovely backside on the edge of his desk. Her smile held an edge. "Last night. When I was there."

James swallowed.

"I saw Dalton. Somehow, though, I missed you. He said you were around." Her gaze pierced his. "I didn't see you...around."

"It's a big place."

"It's a small place."

"It was crowded."

"You weren't there, were you?"

He glared at her. "Yes, I was."

"Until ten?"

"Ten-thirty."

She straightened, planting her hands on her hips. "What about the night before last, when you couldn't take the time to order from the Ming Palace because you had plans with Dalton?"

"I—well..." Actually, he'd snuck down to the corner deli, ordered a Reuben, then ate the sandwich quietly in his apartment. "I just wanted to be alone that night."

"And the night before that when I asked you to come with me, Gwen and Fedora to a play?"

"I made dinner at home and watched ESPN."

"So you lied."

"I—" Suddenly realizing what a slimeball he'd been—even to his own mother—James bowed his head. "Yes."

"Did I push you too hard to go?"

"No."

"Did you feel as though it was part of your job to go?"

"No." He jumped to his feet. "Dammit, Lily, I'm already quitting. You don't have anything to pressure me with."

Her eyes grew watery. "So you lied…so you could avoid me."

This wasn't going at all the way he'd planned. Why had he been so juvenile to avoid her, rather than just explaining that he was running from his attraction to her? Why couldn't he make himself admit that even now? "I just don't need you to entertain me after work," he said lamely. "I have a life beyond you."

"You most certainly do." She spun around and stalked away, slamming the door behind her.

James braced his hands against his desk, his head pounding, his heart contracting. He'd hurt her. Dammit, he was just trying to save himself, and he'd hurt her in the process.

His phone rang, and he snatched the receiver off the hook. "James Chamberlin."

"Hey, buddy, it's me," Dalton said, his voice rusty. "Listen, I'm running out to the office. Overslept. You need to know I saw Lily last night."

James sighed. "Did you really?"

8

THE SUN STREAMING through the windows of her workroom, Lily studied her latest shoe samples. The hot-pink, fur-trimmed, patent-leather sling back was the prize of the group. But the checkerboard, medium pink-and-yellow pump was a close second.

Carlotta would love them. They fit her whimsical line to perfection.

So why wasn't she happy? Why wasn't she relieved she'd made it through the crisis? Why didn't the relief and satisfaction from a job well done suffuse her body?

James.

It was all his fault. That sneaky, underhanded—

She wanted to be mad at him for lying to her, for deliberately avoiding her, but she couldn't work up her temper. She was too busy nursing her ego. Obviously, he wasn't nearly as curious about the sudden sparks between them as she was. She'd decided earlier in the week that if she spent more time with him, she'd either figure out his draw, or decide she'd gone temporarily insane. But that man just wouldn't cooperate.

What else was new?

Playing matchmaker to his parents wasn't going anywhere, either. In fact, her designs were the only thing she felt sure about these days. Personal life: oh for two; business: one to nothing, or actually, three to nothing, if she counted all the Spectacular's collections.

Conclusion? Concentrate on business. Retreat from personal stuff—at least for the moment.

Maybe he's just not interested. You're not his type. Not his cup of tea. Not his "thang."

He was a man, so he responded to her physical presence. But he obviously had no interest in taking things further. They didn't have the same goals, outlooks or personalities.

Get over it, girl.

"Lily, I—" Garnet stopped just inside the room, her wide gaze fixed on the shoes. "Oh. My. God."

Lily held up her hand. "Touch them and die."

Naturally, Garnet ignored the warning. She touched the tip of the stiletto. "But they're perfect. I'm going to Diamond Masterson's coming-out party in two weeks. I have this dress—"

Lily stepped between her receptionist and the shoes. "Diamond?"

Garnet rolled her eyes. "Her dad owns a jewelry store on East Forty-eighth."

"Ah." Lily crossed her arms over her chest. "You can't have these shoes."

Garnet strained to look around her. "Lily…please." She actually dropped to her knees. "I have to have them. And you promised me a pair, remember?"

Despite the lack of commitment to her job, the disrespect toward clients, the penchant for "borrowing" the sample shoes, Lily really liked Garnet. She had a great sense of style. She was young, lovely and enthusiastic. She just needed direction. Lily recalled the last few days she'd spent with Fedora, a lovely, passionate woman. Even if Fedora still refused to speak to her husband, at least she was spreading her wings and finding her own space in the world.

Maybe Garnet needed the same. Besides, Lily owed her for Operation Normal Day.

"You want some shoes for the party? You make them."

Garnet looked away. "I can't."

"Don't even start this discussion that way. You *can*. You just *haven't*. In fact, have you ever tried?"

Garnet shrugged, and for the first time since she'd met her, Lily saw the vulnerability of youth. "Not really."

"But you have ideas."

"Well, yeah. I'd like to design, I guess."

Lily smiled. "Good. Then let's get started."

"Yeah?"

"Yeah." Lily grabbed a sketch pad off the table. "How well do you draw?"

Garnet wrinkled her nose. "Not very well."

Lily tossed the sketch pad aside. "Great, then you can use this new computer program James and Gwen came up with." They crossed the room to the computer station. "I like the aesthetic feel of a pencil in my hand, though James assures me the computer will be faster and more efficient." She pursed her lips. Yet another reason to stay away from that man. Fast and efficient in no way related to the creative process.

She let Garnet sit in the computer chair while Lily booted up the computer, then stood behind her.

Garnet eyed the screen with distinct distrust. "Are

you sure we should be doing this? James will have a cow if we mess something up. By the way, what do we do if we do mess something up?"

"We run out of here and pretend we never touched it."

"Works for me." Garnet pointed at the screen, which was covered by a bunch of little pictures. "Which program is it?"

Lily bit her lip. "Hmm…"

Garnet sighed and pointed at the screen again. "Well, this shoe looks like—" She stopped as the computer whirred again.

Lily grabbed her shoulder. "What did you do?"

"Nothing! I just touched the picture—" A graphic of the company logo appeared on the screen, and Garnet smiled. "The screen is touch activated."

"Oh, cool." Actually, Lily sort of recalled James telling her about the touch thing some time back, but she'd been on her way to a party at the time and hadn't paid much attention. She added a long talk with Gwen and her computer-savvy brain to her mental list of familiarizing herself with her business.

More cute little cartoon pictures appeared on the screen, labeled things such as "Style," "Color" and "Material."

"Okay, why don't we start with the style?" Lily tentatively tapped the *style* button, and nearly laughed aloud when the screen changed to show more pictures of different types of shoes. "Who says computers are complicated? And don't you dare roll your eyes."

"Wouldn't dream of it."

"So, what style do you want? Casual sandal? Heeled sandal? Kick-ass pump?"

"Heeled sandal, I think. Something pretty and feminine."

"How long is the dress?"

"Midcalf."

"Excellent." Lily pressed the *heeled sandal* picture, and the screen changed to little pictures of sandals. "Which one?" she asked after studying the styles for several moments.

Garnet frowned. "I like number three and number seven."

"Hmmph. Mr. Brilliantly Efficient didn't think of everything, did he?"

"Oh, look. There's another page." Garnet pressed the *next page* button, and they found even more styles. After a few more pages, Garnet spotted the perfect one.

They went on to colors and pattern, materials and textures. Garnet *oohed* and *aahed* while Lily grew more and more impressed. It was like looking through a catalog, except without real pages. The computer would never replace her sketching process, but when they pressed the picture of a little printer and a perfect replica of the shoe they'd created slid out, Lily couldn't help but giggle just as shamelessly as Garnet did.

"Wow," Garnet whispered, staring at her first design.

"It's great." And it was. A fun but delicate pastel pink, white and yellow sandal with thin straps that would crisscross around her ankles and lower calves. Perfect for a free-spirited woman. "Now, if only the shoe itself popped out from the computer."

Garnet's eyes widened, as if she'd just realized

she couldn't exactly put on a piece of paper and wear it with her dress. "Diamond's party is two weeks away. Will they be ready in time?"

"You bet. I'll have the production manager rush them through."

Garnet stood and embraced Lily. "Thanks." Then she darted toward the door. "I'm going to take this sketch down to him myself."

A lump actually formed in Lily's throat as Garnet bounced from the room. She doubted her easily distracted receptionist would wander into Starbucks or decide to spontaneously shop during this errand.

James stuck his head around the corner of the doorway. "Garnet's smiling. What did she do?"

"You mean what did she do *wrong*, don't you?"

"Does she do things any other way?"

Lily lifted her chin. "I'll have you know our receptionist has hidden talents as a designer. She just designed herself a pair of shoes."

"As opposed to stealing them off your feet? When did you two become such buddies, anyway?"

"We bonded over touch screens."

His gaze jumped to the computer. "You used the shoe program? How was it?"

"Fast and efficient, Mr. Cynical." She strolled from the room. "I think I'll call it a day. When Garnet gets back, ask her to put the shoes for Carlotta's collection in the storeroom."

"Where are you going?" He kept his gaze on her as she passed him, then added, "In case I need to ask you something later."

"I've got plans." She glanced at him over her

shoulder, pleased when his jaw dropped. "I'll take my cell, so you can reach me. Bye."

She walked down the hall without another word.

SHE WAS IGNORING HIM.

And driving him crazy.

James could hardly believe he was the same man who, less than a week ago, told Dalton he was taking preventive measures to avoid Lily and the temptation she presented. Last week she'd pampered him. She'd flirted with him. She'd smiled at him.

The last few days she'd treated him like an *employee.* And not one she particularly liked, either. He'd told himself all he wanted was for her to go back to her parties and friends and the men who panted after them. Instead, he'd ground his teeth last night when she'd told Garnet—at three-thirty, mind you—she was leaving for a "social commitment," then disappeared into her apartment.

The old Lily would have changed into her stunning outfit, done all her face stuff and perfuming, then sailed through the office to show off her ensemble. Last night she'd quietly left without a word, and he certainly hadn't been invited to see the latest Lily creation.

He was miserable.

He really *had* lost it.

After all his rationalization of their incompatibility, James now realized what a drastic mistake he'd made. What a stupid fool he'd been. What a once-in-a-lifetime opportunity he'd thrown away. He was ready to admit his weakness. And wasn't that the first step to recovery?

No, the first step was getting Lily alone, aroused

and naked. Consequences be damned. "Social commitments," "plans" and "professionalism" be double damned.

His body was way past the point of resistance. Then, when it all fell apart, he and his dad could moan and whine together.

All that was fine and good, he supposed. But aside from his primary problem of dealing with a Lily who was now determined to ignore him, he had another big obstacle, as well.

Teresa.

He couldn't pursue Lily and still see Teresa. They hadn't made promises to each other or anything, it just didn't feel right. It felt like cheating.

And even if he had lost his mind and his natural resistance to the wild and impractical, he hadn't lost his integrity.

So that night he headed to his final date with Teresa. After the movie, he took her back to her apartment and asked if they could talk a minute.

"Sure," she said, stepping back from the door opening. "You want some tea or coffee?"

James went into the living room and sat on the flowery sofa, letting his hands dangle between his knees. *I need a good shot of whiskey.* "No, thanks."

Tucking her legs beneath her, she sat on the opposite end of the sofa. "You've been really quiet all night. What's wrong?"

He shook his head, feeling even worse than he'd anticipated. Teresa was a nice woman. She didn't deserve this. Still, he couldn't pretend any longer.

He looked over at her. "I don't think we should see each other anymore."

Her eyes widened. "Why? I thought we—" She stopped, her eyes filling with tears.

He wanted to hold her, but didn't think she'd want him touching her under the circumstances. "You're a great woman, Teresa. It's just not working out for me."

"But we're so much alike. We have the same goals and outlooks. We agree about our direction in life."

Ah, logic. His old friend. He sighed. "I know."

"This is about Lily, isn't it?"

"I—" He wasn't about to get into that. It seemed too hurtful and inappropriate. "It's about me."

After a few more awkward explanations, James left, found the nearest bar and retreated to its darkest corner. Far away from the laughing crowd, he listened to the blues band and stared guiltily into his martini.

This is about Lily, isn't it?

Though he hadn't admitted anything to Teresa, he could at least be honest with himself. Oh, yeah, this was *completely* about Lily.

He was recklessly throwing away safe and steady for wild uncertainty and conflict. Since his mother was still living with Lily and refusing to speak to her husband except when they were on stage, he wondered if his behavior was genetically inevitable.

He'd wanted to see Lily too much after leaving Teresa, so this was the best place for him. He felt kind of vulnerable at the moment, and he really needed to be strong when he faced her again. She was going to be suspicious about his sudden turnabout, so he had to be subtle in his seduction. He needed to think and plan.

Lily's presence distracted him too much. Her

curves, her scent and her smile all turned his brain to mush. Maybe he could call her. But then, her voice was equally distracting.

James...

He liked the way she said his name. Sometimes soft, sometimes needy, sometimes upbeat.

"James!"

He jerked his head up. And there stood Lily, dressed in a sleek, low-cut black top and jeans with rhinestones down the seams and flanked by Gwen and Kristin.

"I—" He swallowed hard and stood. "Hi."

"You looked kind of lost back here," Lily said, meeting his gaze. "Are you okay?"

She was pissed as hell at him, but she still worried. Compassion. Yet another quality of hers he couldn't resist.

Her scent had enveloped him. The skin between her breasts glistened in the candlelight. He ground his teeth. Subtle wasn't in Lily's vocabulary. No one would blame him for being unable to resist *that*.

James worked up a smile. "I'm fine." He extended his hand. "Join me?"

Gwen and Kristin looked to Lily for direction. Surprisingly, she nodded. They settled at the table with Lily and Kristin on either side and Gwen across from him. With their colorful martinis in yellow, pink and green, they looked like a rainbow of cheer. They were really ruining his depressed mood.

Gwen's icy-blue gaze swept him. "You're certainly the life of the party."

Lily shook her head. "Gwen, don't."

Just like the other night with his mother. She was angry with him, yet she defended him.

Kristin laid her arm across his shoulders. "What's wrong, Jimmy? Your love life bringing you down?"

Lily leaned around him and gave Kristin a sharp look.

Kristin smiled. *"What?"*

Lily kicked him.

"Ow!" James jerked back from the table, rubbing his shin. "Hey, that was *me*, you know."

"Sorry," Lily mumbled, then sipped her drink. "How 'bout those Yankees?"

"It's February, Lily," Gwen said dryly. "The Yankees are probably hanging out at the beach."

Lily flipped her hair over her shoulder. "Excuse me. I'm just trying to make *appropriate*—" she glared at Kristin "—conversation."

"I broke things off with Teresa," James blurted out, then stared into his martini glass as if it had caused his babbling.

Lily looked at him in horror. *"What?"*

It was official. He'd never understand women. She'd flirted with him. She'd kissed him senseless. The other night she'd even told him he should grab things as they come. And now she was *upset* he'd broken off his relationship with another woman?

"What a shame," Kristin said, smirking at Lily.

Lily made a slicing motion across her throat.

Ignoring her, Kristin went on, "That's so…"

"Convenient?" Gwen said, raising her eyebrows.

"I was going to say unfortunate."

Lily drummed her fingernails against the table. "I wish you guys wouldn't say anything at all."

"It *is* unfortunate," Kristin said. "Our poor, dear James so obviously in pain."

"I wouldn't say I'm in pain—exactly."

Kristin patted his hand. "Of course you are, sweetie. This is the woman you were going to marry, after all."

James flicked his gaze to Lily, who'd grabbed the drink menu and was holding it in front of her face. "I had no idea my love life was such interesting conversation."

Kristin flushed. "Lily might have mentioned the whole wedding thing."

"But just in passing," Gwen added.

"What happened, James, dear? I was already picking out my dress for the nuptials."

"I didn't say I was *going* to marry her, just that she was the *kind* of woman I'd *like* to marry."

"I don't see why you were so hot to get married in the first place," Lily said, setting down the menu.

"I'm not getting married!"

Her eyes brightened. "Ever?"

"I will get married. Just not right now. And I don't understand why you're so against marriage."

"Doesn't look like a gaggle of fun to me."

He wasn't up to sparring with her, and he certainly didn't want to be reminded how different they were. "Lily, everything in life is not fun."

"Why do you want to get married if it's not fun?" Gwen asked, frowning.

"It is fun—some of the time. Just not all the time. You have to work at a lasting relationship. It doesn't just happen."

Wide-eyed, the women stared at him.

"Will you marry me?" Kristin and Gwen asked at the same time.

Lily dropped her gaze and sipped her drink.

This night wasn't going at all as he'd planned. He'd finally admitted to himself that he couldn't go forward in his life plan without giving in to his attraction to Lily. He'd given up on a perfectly lovely woman so that he was free and clear to pursue her. He'd decided to ignore his conscience, which kept warning him he would come out on the bad end of a volatile relationship with Lily. He'd started on a plan of seduction.

But the woman he wanted was ignoring him.

Kristin prodded his arm. "So, what happened between you and the teacher?"

"I—" Why the hell did he start this discussion? "It was a mutual decision."

Kristin made a tsking sound. "No sparks, I bet."

James started to interrupt, mainly because he didn't like the fact that Kristin had nailed the reason so perfectly, but she kept rolling along.

"Happened to me last year. I met this guy I thought was perfect for me. Stable, good-looking, but *bor-ring.*" She flung her hand out. "Zippo fire. I guess you're going to get right back at it, though."

"Back at what?"

"Dating. Finding Miss Right. I'll bet there's not much of a social scene in Connecticut. Lots of cows and chowder, but not many single ladies."

Looking as if she'd rather be anywhere else but at this particular table, Lily stared at the ceiling.

Since he'd heard the same argument—almost word for word—from Lily several times, it seemed as though his love life had been discussed by these three extensively. He'd suspected as much when Lily had first begun her flattering-and-pampering scheme.

With these three working together, it was no wonder he'd lost his resistance.

"How much time do you have left in the city?" Kristin asked, leaning forward.

"Ah…just over two months."

"Not much time." She pressed her lips together. "Hmm. Girls, should we volunteer to help him? Now, who do we know—"

Gwen's chair scraped against the floor as she jumped to her feet. "I need another drink. Anybody else?"

Kristin glanced into her half-full glass. "I'm fine."

James drained his glass and stood. "I could use another, but I'll get the waitress." He extended his hand. "Sit back down, Gwen."

She shook her head. "She'll never see us back here." She gave Kristin a pointed look. "Kristin would love to come with me."

"No, I—"

"Don't you have to use the bathroom?" Gwen asked.

"No, I—"

Gwen grabbed her by the arm. "I do." She pulled a reluctant Kristin off with her.

Group bathroom breaks. Another aspect of women he'd never understand. As he returned to his seat, his gaze slid to Lily. She was back to staring into her glass and frowning.

"What's with those two?"

"They're giving us a minute alone together."

"How do you know—" He stopped. "Never mind. Do we need a moment alone together?" He really didn't have his seduction plan down pat yet. He'd rather have another day or two of preparation.

"I'm sorry about you and Teresa," Lily said softly, just as the band began a moody sax ballad.

"It's fine."

"Was she really upset?"

"A bit." He recalled the stunned look on Teresa's face and felt like a jerk all over again. "I think she was mostly surprised."

"Are *you* really upset?"

"No. I just feel guilty."

Her eyes widened. "You do?"

He shrugged. "A little. We hadn't been dating long. I just—I feel like I disappointed her."

"Oh." She looked around awkwardly.

He was losing her attention. And who could blame her? He'd kept telling her she wasn't on his schedule and continued to deny that he felt anything toward her, other than as an employee and friend.

James angled his body toward Lily. She looked really spectacular, her shoulders gleaming in the low light. And, for once, he ignored his conscience's warning that he was getting too close to her. A seduction could hardly begin until he explained himself. "But I couldn't keep seeing her when I realized I was interested in someone else."

Her gaze zipped back to his. "Who?"

"*You.*"

"I thought I wasn't part of your *plan.*"

"Yeah, well…" He felt his face heat. "That was a pretty stupid thing to say. I also shouldn't have lied to you about my plans with Dalton."

"No, you shouldn't have." She sighed. "But I shouldn't have acted like such a baby and ignored you in retaliation. Besides, I assume I drove you to avoid me."

He slid his hand over hers. "You didn't. I—" Well, he couldn't say he hadn't wanted to avoid her, because he had. He'd pretended their relationship hadn't been changing over the last few weeks. He'd denied their attraction. But now he had the opportunity to get everything out in the open. Ignoring his feelings certainly hadn't done him any good. "I avoided you because I was afraid to be tempted by you. I didn't *want* to want you."

Lily's eyes widened. She grinned. "But you do now? Want me, I mean?"

"Oh, yeah." And, wow, did it feel good to finally admit it out loud. He might be making a mistake, giving in to the unknown, stepping deliberately into the fire Lily generated, but caution was an afterthought. It was a risk he was willing to take.

"It's been a weird couple of weeks," she admitted. "I haven't exactly been honest with you either about what's been happening between us." Her gaze softened as she met his eyes. "I didn't expect to want to kiss you, much less like it."

"But you did? Like it, I mean?"

She laughed at his echo of her words. "Oh, yeah."

"No more denying. You feel something, you want something, you tell me."

"Deal."

He leaned closer to her. Even in the smoky club, he could detect her distinct, sexy scent. "Does this mean you'll kiss me again?"

Her gaze burned into his as she slid her finger

around the rim of her martini glass. "Does this mean you'll let me?"

"We're back," Kristin announced, trotting toward the table with Gwen just behind her.

Lily glanced up at her friends. "Oh, goody."

A phone rang, and the ladies all fumbled for their bags, trying to figure out whose cell it was. Lily flipped open her phone—covered in pink rhinestones—and announced, "It's me."

"Hi, Fabian." She paused. "Uh-huh. You're kidding! Of course we'll come. Save us a seat." A pleased smile on her face, she snapped her phone closed. "Guess who's playing at Salsa Caliente tonight?"

Gwen and Kristin leaned forward. "Who?"

"José Lambino."

The girls squealed.

James grinned. Only Lily could find a singer named José Lambino. He wondered if he was a crossdresser, Elvis impersonator, gay cabaret singer, or a guy with a singing poodle.

Lily turned to him as she hooked her purse on her arm and stood. "He's half Mexican and half Italian, so he sings Italian standards in Spanish."

Kristin's eyes lit. "You should hear his 'Volare.' It's a classic."

"I'll bet," he said.

"Come on, James," Gwen said, rising.

He hesitated. He wanted to be with Lily, but they'd probably be out all night, and he had tons of work to get through tomorrow.

Lily raised her eyebrows—a challenge if he ever saw one. "Aren't you coming?"

9

"Yeah," James said, rising from his seat. "I'm coming."

Lily was proud of herself for the demure smile she sent his way. "Okay. Let's go, then."

"I'll pay the bill and meet you guys outside."

Lily broadened her smile. "Thanks."

His eyes darkened, turning hungry. Definitely a better look than the morose one she'd first encountered. "I'll be right there," he said.

As she turned away, she grabbed Kristin's arm. She couldn't pretend for another second that this whole night hadn't both excited and shaken her. "What's with you and the fake sympathy over James and Teresa's breakup? We plotted this very thing."

"James looks like a man perfectly capable of making his own decisions."

Kristin's reassurance made her feel a bit better. She'd talked about doing it, of course, but she hadn't followed through. In fact, she'd sent him on to his date the night Carlotta had dropped her color bombshell.

Still, even if she didn't deliberately cause problems between James and Teresa, he *had* broken up with Teresa because of her. The whole idea made her feel happy and guilty at the same time.

Much like James's reaction, she guessed.

He really does want me. He'd actually admitted he was attracted to her. And he was going along on an adventure without looking as though he might be tortured when he got there.

Gwen, who'd obviously caught the conversation, said, "He wants you, girl."

She grinned at her friends. "Yeah, I think he does."

"His eyes lit up like the city skyline when you walked up to the table," Kristin added.

Lily's body warmed at the thought. Could this thing with James actually be happening? *No more denying.* The man drove her absolutely crazy. Just when she'd decided to let him go, he'd done a one-eighty on her.

"So what's with the big turnaround?" Gwen asked as if reading her mind.

"I'm not sure. One minute he's denying everything, then outright avoiding me, then the next he's flirting with me."

"You're both thinking too much," Gwen said, always practical. "Jump in the sack and get it over with."

That had been Lily's first impulse, as well, but given how well she knew James, how closely they worked together, she wondered if things could be that simple.

They pushed through the door held open by the bouncer out into the rainy, chilly night. Lily drew her coat tighter around her. Her internal battle had twisted her stomach into knots, but it was comforting to know she hadn't been the only one struggling.

They flagged down a cab and had all squeezed inside just as James exited the restaurant. He sat in the front, and Lily stared at the back of his head for most of the trip as her buddies chatted about the recent scandal of some senator caught in an uptown hotel room with a young pop star—who most certainly was not his proper New England wife.

What *had* brought about this one-eighty? She'd been a temptation to him compromising his professional ethics; he wanted to pretend their attraction didn't exist. She wasn't part of his *plan*.

But tonight he'd sat in the back of a darkened club looking sad and alone. He'd tolerated her friends' personal questions. He'd apologized for avoiding her. He'd leaned toward her and smelled like a sensual dream.

Maybe he *was* the perfect man. Even her friends thought so. Charming and sweet. Controlled, but semiadventurous. Efficient and loyal.

She laid her head back against the seat. Even aside from the immediate needs of her libido, a relationship with him could be the best thing for her.

Until he left, of course.

Oh, yeah, Lily, thoughts like that will put you in the party mood.

The cab pulled up to the entrance of the club, which was, unbelievably, deserted. Lily shook her head. She loved Broadway as much as anybody, but it was the off-Broadway—okay, maybe in José's case, off-off-off-Broadway—productions she gravitated toward. New people, new ideas, new formats.

James helped each of them from the cab, then paid the driver, and she made a mental note to herself to repay him. It wasn't his responsibility to foot the bill for their night out.

They passed the red velvet ropes, which were deserted. Then breezed by the bar—also deserted. They found Fabian and his trio date—this time brunettes—in the center of the room, facing the stage. The prime table. Probably because nearly every other table was also available.

Shameful. José was a genius. The next big thing.

"Lily!" Fabian rose as they approached him. He extended his hand to the table beside him. "I saved you a seat."

Lily kissed his cheek, then waved at his dates. "Thanks. You're a doll."

They flung their coats over their chairs, then ordered drinks. Impulsively, because she felt so bad for the club and wanted to make sure somebody knew José had loyal fans, Lily ordered an expensive bottle of champagne.

Eventually, she ordered several.

James gave her a cautious look only once, and Lily took that opportunity to whisper to him, "What else is money for?"

She was sure he could come up with several ideas, and she could, too. But she just couldn't stand the thought of a party that should be happening and wasn't. She'd dreamed of going to hip nightspots and buying the house a round back in Iowa, when she wasn't sure she'd ever get to the big city. She wasn't blowing her chance now.

In the middle of José's second set, James approached her as she leaned against the railing separating the dance floor from the tables. "The bartender wants to know if you're buying everyone another round."

Lily glanced around the club. *Holy hell, where had*

all these people come from? "Oh, they're cut off. There were twelve people here an hour ago."

"Apparently, they called twelve people, who called twelve people…"

"Who can all buy their own drinks."

"And I used to worry that we never thought alike." He nodded toward the stage. "He's pretty good, though I can't understand a word he's saying."

"You don't have to understand. Just accept."

He raised one eyebrow. "Do I?"

"Not everything in life is predictable and planable."

"I shouldn't try to control the uncontrollable."

She smiled. "Just go with the moment. Occasionally."

"My mother went with the moment recently, remember?"

She knew James was worried about his parents' relationship. Not living under the same roof was certainly a bad sign, she guessed. But she also knew they were the most in-love couple she'd ever met. They wouldn't—*couldn't*—stay away from each other for long. "She'll go back to him."

"I'm not so sure. But even if they do, it'll just start all over again."

"What will start all over again?"

"The fights, the drama, the make-ups, the calls to me to play negotiator."

Lily snagged a glass of water off Fabian's table just beside them. She'd figured James had struggled with Fedora's sense of drama, but she'd never expected him to share his feelings with her. "They're both strong people. Of course they're going to fight."

"I just don't understand why they can't sit down and have a rational conversation about their problems."

"Not all problems are rational." She drank from the glass. The smoky clubs had completely dried out her throat. "This one certainly isn't. Deep down, your mother knows she shouldn't try to make you feel guilty about leaving. She knows your father is right. And that's driving her crazy."

He lifted his hands. "See what I mean?"

"She can't change what she feels." She remembered something about the night that Fedora had shown up, though. A point she hadn't pressed James about. "Did you really think I'd plot with your mother to keep you here?"

He shrugged. "You two are so alike. It's something she would do. Correction, something she *is* doing."

Lily glared at him. "She is not."

"Why do you think she's staying with you?"

"She happens to like me, James."

"She does, yes. She's also showing me—look what will happen if you retire. My marriage will fall apart. Lily will have me dating dozens of men in no time."

"I don't date dozens of men."

"Sure you do."

"Jealous?"

"Intensely."

"*Really?*" She stepped closer to him, looking up at him and deciding she liked this promise of honesty they'd made. She liked knowing she could express herself with him, touch him, and he wouldn't run in the other direction. *You feel something, you want something...* "Well, you also ought to know I have no intention of using your mother to get to you." She drew her finger down the center of his chest. "However...I have other ways of fighting dirty."

"You make a man want to beg for mercy."

Lily licked her lips. "You won't get any. Mercy, that is."

He stared at her and braced his hands on her hips.

"Want a sip?" She held out the glass. "I'm asking because your eyes are glued to my glass."

"They're glued to your lips."

Her heart hammered. A responsive James was something to behold. And touch...

She set the glass aside, then linked her arms around his neck, bringing her face within inches of his. His warm breath brushed her skin. His body stiffened. His eyes darkened.

Clients, her friends, an entire club of people surrounded them, but Lily focused only on James. *No more denying.* She knew she'd embarrass him if she kissed him the way she wanted to. They'd turned a corner tonight, and she didn't want to jeopardize that. Besides, she thought with a teasing smile, there were some advantages to drawing out the moment.

She flicked her tongue against his bottom lip.

His heart jumped against his chest.

Not deepening the kiss, but not backing up either, she said, "The shoe program is really cool."

His hands flexed against her hips. He shifted his stance, and his erection brushed her stomach. "You want to talk about *shoes?*"

She searched his gaze. "You don't?"

"Well—" He glanced around, and she could see regret slip into his eyes. He sighed. "Sure. Let's talk about shoes."

She stroked her fingers through the hair behind his ear. "I was just—"

"Do I have to talk coherently? I can't think straight when you do that."

The heat in his eyes made her belly flutter. "Think of it as multitasking. I see you do that all the time."

He swallowed. "I'll try."

"Now, what was I talking about?"

"Shoes, I think."

"Oh, right. The program. Garnet did really well with it."

"You were nice to help her. She's really proud of her design. She actually got a message right yesterday."

"She has good instincts. Maybe she's just not suited to office work."

"Not everyone is."

"Why are you?"

He lifted his shoulders in a shrug. "Just lucky, I guess."

"I guess you didn't want to follow your parents in the theater?"

"Hell, no. In the early days, we never knew where, or if, the next paycheck was coming. We—really me—juggled rent and bills. We moved around all the time. The apartment was always filled with chaotic people."

She'd suspected all this, but she was glad he'd shared his frustration with her. She always burdened him with her worries, but he never opened up to her. Maybe because she never invited him to. "So you learned to bring order to the world."

"I *had* to."

"When I first became a designer, my life was exactly like yours." She paused and considered the chaotic-people thing. "Okay, maybe it still is."

"But you managed to focus. You're a great success."

"Thanks to you."

James stroked her cheek. "You did it. I just put everything in neat and orderly columns."

The pride in his eyes—pride for her—made her heart flip.

"Maybe we did it together," she whispered, then pressed her lips to his.

Lily made herself move her mouth slowly, deliberately over his. She gripped the lapels of his jacket, pulling him against her, inhaling the spicy, seductive scent that clung to his skin and clothes. His mouth was warm, his lips soft.

She wanted to experience so much more with him than just a night or two of passion. They might be opposites in many ways, but he understood her, supported her like no one in her life ever had. *God, I hope I don't screw this up.*

He moaned quietly as she pulled away. "Lily…"

"Thank you! *Gracias* and *adiós!*"

Lily turned in time to see José waving to the crowd as he jogged off the stage. And before she could turn back to James, Fabian had embraced her. Then her friends surrounded her, and within minutes they were all bundled into cabs and headed home. Of course, Fabian had organized the taxis, so she and James were in separate cars, even though they were the only two people who lived in the same building.

By the time the cab arrived at her address, she'd been up and down a dozen different streets to drop off the others, so James was already there. Waiting for her.

He took her hand and assisted her out of the cab, and the scent of him again washed over her. Her head felt somewhat light as she stood on the sidewalk and he paid the driver.

They were finally alone.

Her stomach fluttered with nerves. What would he say? Or *do*? What should she say? Or *do*?

This is ridiculous. You're a grown woman. You want to have sex with this guy? Just do it.

But, boy, oh boy, did "have sex" absolutely *not* encompass the depth of their relationship. They were friends, boss and employee—well sorta, she really considered them partners. James had made it clear from the beginning that he wasn't willing to mix his business and personal life, definitely not to the degree of becoming lovers anyway. Maybe Mr. Plan It All Out was right.

He pulled her coat tighter around her, then took her arm and escorted her into the building. "The show was good. José has lots of energy. I can see why you've become a fan. Thanks for inviting me."

"You're welcome," she mumbled, feeling slightly nauseous with anxiety. This *never* happened to her. She didn't agonize over decisions. She went with instinct, impulse, her gut. At the moment, though, her gut was twisted into knots and incapable of forming a coherent response.

The ride in the elevator was mostly silent, and she wondered about his thoughts. Was he nervous as well? Did he expect her to make the first move?

"I'm dropping you off at your door, Lily," he said as they walked down the hall.

She swallowed, not sure if that was good or bad news. "You are?"

He stopped just outside the entrance to her apartment, and brushed her hair back from her face. "Yes, and not because I don't want you to invite me in, but because if you do, I'll accept, and if we're alone at all tonight there will be no going back." James stroked her jaw with the pad of his thumb. "I know it's stupid, but I'd rather not start the evening with one woman and finish it with another."

Lily blinked. Her heart swelled. *Wow.*

"You think I'm nuts, but—"

She laid her finger over his lips. "I think you're the most honorable man I know." Leaning forward, she lightly pressed her mouth to his, then slipped inside her apartment.

LILY STOOD on the ladder adding the final touch of mustard-yellow paint to the giant, twenty-foot-high arch in the middle of the Spectacular set, which a small army had built in the corner of her supply warehouse. She couldn't remember the last time she'd painted anything. During her teenage years, there'd always been a barn or fence to paint, and she'd sworn she'd never look at another bucket of paint again.

But she'd forgotten the simple satisfaction of watching something change so quickly, so easily. The mindless strokes, the way your thoughts wandered. In her case, of course, they'd wandered to James and her unfulfilled desire. Maybe *that's* why she was so anxious to expend restless energy.

"My people need the paint they ordered, Mr. Williams," she heard James say suddenly.

She peeked over the arch to see him talking on his cell phone and striding across the warehouse floor. Her heart immediately picked up speed.

"The show is just over a week away. We have sets to build."

He paused, and shivers bounded down Lily's spine. His voice was so...commanding. She got hot all over when he took charge.

Oh, girl, you need help.

"And I'm a very pissed-off man," he continued to whomever had obviously made the mistake of not giving him what he wanted. "We came to your company on the recommendation of a colleague, but I can assure you that if I don't get my paint in less than two hours, the lack of future recommendations will be the least of your worries." James paused again, listening. "I'm calling Home Depot in one hour and fifty-five minutes." He disconnected and slid the phone into his pocket. "Idiot. How difficult is it to mix some paint?"

In the last month, she knew he'd ordered lumber, steel, glass, mirrors, screws, electrical wires, nails, lights and a dozen other supplies. Invitations had been sent to hundreds of people. Three major clothing designers plus her and all their employees, suppliers and craftpeople were working overtime to get their fashions ready. The media had been sent press releases.

She sincerely doubted he'd let some idiotic hardware-store guy screw up his well-ordered plan.

Lily supposed he wouldn't have to hassle with any of this much longer. Pretty soon, he'd wake up to fresh air and quiet in the country. Cows and puppies lolling in the meadows. He could swap gossip at his café or drink a latte over the morning paper.

By contrast, her business seemed like a tornado of trouble.

He continued walking toward the set, and she simply sighed as she watched him move, dressed to perfection in a navy suit, his dark hair brushed back from his strong face. She marveled that she'd spent the last several months with him and never taken the time to study him. Had she been blind? Crazy? Why had she wasted her time on losers like Brian when she could have had James?

She'd let his professional distance be a barrier between them. And maybe that had been for the best. What would she have done if she'd managed to seduce him, only to have their relationship fall apart a few weeks or months later? He'd have left and—

He was leaving, anyway. Hell, she'd wasted *way* too much time.

And when he leaves you? Not just the job, but you?

"Maybe I'll leave him," she whispered.

But for some reason, she couldn't picture that happening, and a different kind of chill slid down her spine. She'd spent a lot of time recently getting back in touch with the details of her business. She had Gwen's assurances that she'd be her on-call computer consultant, her accountant had promised to give her extra support. Her business would survive if James left, but would *she*?

"How's it going, gang?" he asked the crew.

He got a few waves and a few grumbles. Lily also waved from her perch atop the arch, but he didn't see her at first. His head turned back to the runway for a moment, then he did a double take and craned his neck back.

"Lily?"

She waved at him with her brush. "Hi, James."

Frowning, he walked toward her. "I thought you were having lunch with Gwen."

"I was, but I decided to come by here and see if I could help. They gave me a paintbrush, and here I am."

He walked around the arch to the ladder's base and looked up at her.

She smiled until she realized that from his angle he could probably see right up her orange minidress.

Of course, she was wearing lacy thong underwear, so that wasn't necessarily a bad thing.

He should have looked away. He shouldn't be staring. She couldn't imagine the James of two weeks ago blatantly staring up her dress.

But he didn't move.

Sweat beaded along her lower back. Would he like to slide his hand up her leg? How about see the matching bra?

Acting as if she had no idea she was exposing herself to him, she extended her arm toward the arch. "I'm a pretty good painter, don't you think?"

"Uh... Ah... Yep."

She planted one hand on her hip. "Are you okay?"

"Uh... Ah... Yep."

She giggled. Then it occurred to her that she was flirting with the man from twenty feet away. Not exactly where she did her best work.

She started down the ladder. "You look kind of pale."

When she reached the ground, he finally moved—grabbing her hand to assist her off the ladder. She stood before him barefoot, wearing a one-shoulder orange dress, her hair in a messy ponytail. She probably looked ridiculous. Still, she liked the look in his eyes. Kind of stunned. Hungry.

"Are you sure you're okay?"

"No." He pulled her to the side, away from the arch and the activity around the rest of the set. "You shouldn't be standing on a ladder in that dress."

She waved her hand in dismissal, pretending she didn't know what he was talking about. "I didn't want to take the time to go home and change. We're all working. Nobody's paying attention to me." *Well, almost nobody.*

"I think you ought to stick with projects a little closer to the ground."

"I don't know what anybody could possibly see—" She broke off and pretended to look surprised. "You looked."

"I—"

"You looked up my dress."

"Hell, Lily, it was hard not to."

She angled her head. "See anything you liked?"

James captured her hand and pulled her toward him. He wiped her cheek, then turned his thumb around to show her a yellow paint smudge. "I certainly did."

She went still. She hadn't expected such a direct answer. *No more denying.* "Really?"

His gaze searched hers. "Oh, yeah."

Then he smiled.

And Lily knew she loved him. Oh, boy, she really *loved* him.

She respected him, valued his opinion, his ability to run a business. She loved his sense of responsibility and honor. She loved that he got impatient when things didn't go the way he wanted. She loved that he respected his mother and wanted her to be happy. She loved his understanding and patience. She loved his eyes and the silky feel of his hair.

She just—she just *loved* him.

He slid his thumb along her jaw. "What?"

Laying her hand on his chest, she shook her head. "Nothing. I just—" She couldn't speak. The words and emotions clogged her throat. She'd only wanted to enjoy him, share something more with him than sales projections and the planning calendar, assuage her desire. To have fun—simple, uncomplicated fun.

"I just appreciate you," she said finally, knowing everything had just gotten a whole lot more complicated. "You've done so much for me, been there for me when no one else has."

"We've been there for each other."

Not for much longer. Her heart was clogging her throat, but she wanted to understand why this had happened. Her heart wasn't supposed to settle on one guy. Not *now*. Especially not the one guy who wanted exactly what she didn't—to escape as far away from the life she led as possible to a quiet life on a farm.

"Do you think we work so well together because we're so different?" she asked. "That we balance each other?"

He cocked his head as if he'd never thought about

their relationship in that way. "Yeah. I guess. Let's talk about it over dinner tonight."

Dinner? She couldn't eat. In fact, she felt slightly nauseous.

"Come on. I'll make paella."

The mention of the seafood-infused Spanish dish piqued Lily's interest. She didn't really cook these days. When she'd first come to the city, she'd existed on microwave meals, ham sandwiches and mushy spaghetti. Maybe that's why she'd started eating out as soon as she could afford to. "*You* can make paella?"

"I wanted to be a chef at one time, remember?"

Oh, she remembered, all right. She remembered he was leaving. The only way she'd get to see him after he quit was if she drove to Connecticut for a damn cappuccino. She was going to have a serious discussion with her heart later and put her hormones back in charge.

"Fedora and I were supposed to go out," she said.

His eyes dimmed, then refocused. "Can you postpone?"

She'd have to come up with something good. Fedora wanted Lily to help her keep her son in the city, but she wasn't sure how his mother would feel about her trying to seduce him. "I guess."

"Around seven. Will you come?"

She couldn't have resisted that look in his eyes for the world. "I'll be there."

10

LILY ARRIVED at his apartment with nerves and a bottle of wine. She'd considered champagne, but thought the cork popping might be *too* apropos.

She'd spent the rest of the afternoon talking herself out of loving him. She was simply here to enjoy herself. Once this vibrating, aching need was satisfied, she'd be back to normal. By next week she'd be interested in another man, and she could renew her campaign to keep James around for strictly business reasons.

She believed almost none of that rationale, but felt somehow comforted that she could temporarily delude herself.

After babbling about work to Fedora, she'd sent her off with Gwen and Kristin, which added a whole different element to the evening. It all felt clandestine, forbidden. Exciting.

Unless her friends took Fedora to a raunchy strip club and James never spoke to her again for corrupting his mother.

He opened the door mere seconds after she'd rung, making her think he'd been standing nearby.

"Hi," he said as he stepped back from the opening to let her pass.

He was wearing jeans, no shoes and a white shirt with *several* buttons undone. He looked casual and comfortable. Extremely sexy and…hey, where'd he get that tan? They hadn't seen warmth or sun for weeks. Had his skin always been that swarthy? And why should she find that sexy? Tanning was very bad.

He raised his eyebrows. "Are you coming in?"

Trying to play it cool, she glanced down the hall as if a better offer might come along. "Yeah, sure." She rolled her shoulders, then walked inside. She'd never been nervous around James. Actually, she wasn't nervous around anybody, but she'd only been inside his apartment once, just after he moved in, so surely that had to be the reason for this stomach-rolling silliness.

Because she couldn't possibly be worried about the night to come. It was a dinner date. That's it. Simple. She'd had many. Nothing to be anxious about.

Seeing his taupe sofa, glass-topped tables, pictures of their first big fashion show together, photos of his parents, big-screen TV and burning wood in the fireplace, a sense of intimacy moved through her that she'd never felt before. She had the urge to lie down on the rug in front of the fireplace and never leave.

Okay, maybe this wasn't going to be as simple as she thought.

Lily handed James the wine bottle. "I brought this."

His smile went straight to his eyes. "Thanks, but I put champagne on ice. Is that okay?"

She swallowed. "Sure. Have you been to the tanning bed?"

"No, of course not," he said as he set the wine on the kitchen counter.

She breathed a sigh of relief. Why had she

thought that? She couldn't picture James going to the tanning salon. She was just off balance, though she couldn't imagine why. This was just a dinner date. No big deal.

"You have pictures of us in here," she said, pointing at the two photos of them on the end table between the sofa and love seat.

He glanced at them, then back at her. "One is our first big show, remember?"

"Yeah. Carlotta called and—"

"No." He stepped close to her. "Well, yes. But Carlotta's not who I remember. I remember you," he whispered. "I remember you strutting into that exhibition hall like you owned it. You wore a tan suit with a black blouse and tan-and-black sling backs."

Of course he remembered what she wore. There was a picture of her right there on the table.

"Your skirt was so short, the show's director had to help you pull up your thigh-high stockings before she introduced you onstage at the end."

She stared up at him. He'd watched *that?*

"I remember the way you understood Carlotta and her nerves. The way you brought smiles to even the jaded models' faces. I remember you wobbling, just a bit, before you walked out onstage. I caught your arm and steadied you."

"That's an incredibly detailed rundown of that show."

He smiled. "Isn't it?"

Was he really *that* detailed? Her stomach continued its odd dance, so she brushed her hand down her short black jacket. Beneath, she'd worn a kelly-green silk tank top, straight black skirt and green sandals.

Her panties had shamrocks all over them. As usual, had she gone too far?

He brushed his thumb across her cheek. "You have a shamrock on your face."

"It's a temporary tattoo. It's nearly Saint Pat's Day, you know." She actually had another one someplace else on her body and hoped he'd get to see that one as well. "I was tired of pink."

Slowly, a smile—a sexy smile that had her stomach flipping—spread across his face. "I'll bet."

She bit her lip. "It's too much."

"It's not. It's perfect." He pressed his lips to her forehead. "You're perfect."

Her heart hammered. "No, I'm not. I'm impatient and flighty. I have a horrible temper. I change my mind every three seconds—just ask my friends. I'm lousy at making decisions. I can't organize anything. I—"

"Lily." He didn't say her name so much as he breathed it, and her stomach finally settled. "I don't care about any of that. I just want to be with you."

She searched his eyes and found tenderness and understanding. "Oh. Okay."

He pressed his lips to hers—a brief caress that was over too soon. "Let me pour you a glass of champagne."

They ate paella by candlelight. They talked about work, then nothing about work. They laughed and flirted. Lily found her defenses sliding. The idea that she didn't love him was a faded memory, a defense she'd tried to raise. With zero success.

When he asked her to dance, she floated into his arms. She clung to him, her arms wrapped around his neck. His very presence made her dizzy with anticipation. She wanted so much to be part of him, for him to take her into his confidence. To trust her with his thoughts and his world.

"We've danced a lot lately," he said against her ear.

"I guess we have."

"I don't want to stop with just a dance tonight."

Her pulse jumped. She leaned back a bit to meet his gaze. The look in his eyes was intense, focused, but lovely. Especially since he didn't seem inclined to fax or call or organize anything. "Me, neither."

Then his mouth captured hers. She closed her eyes, concentrating on the sensations. The drop in her stomach, the tingling through her veins, the warmth of his skin.

She drank it all in, because no matter how much she wanted to believe she was enough, that she could hold him to the city, she knew she was lying to herself. He'd made his decision. He was leaving. Nothing she did now or in the future would make a difference.

And she just didn't care.

She wanted to touch him, know the feel of his skin, the warmth of his body. She wanted to enjoy him while it lasted, to hold the moment tightly in her greedy fist.

He slid his mouth along her jaw, down her throat. She gripped the front of his shirt as a stab of desire punched its way through her body.

She pressed her face against the base of his throat and inhaled the spicy, clean scent that enveloped him. She delighted in the warmth of his touch. Though he'd made no move to remove her clothes yet—damn, the man was patient—she couldn't wait to touch his skin. She slid her hands along the seam of his shirt, fumbling with the remaining buttons. Her breath heaved in and out of her lungs. She wanted to get closer. *Had* to get closer.

When she finally parted the shirt and ran her palms over his bare chest, she closed her eyes in pleasure. She recalled the night she'd found him asleep in his office, when she'd longed to slide just one finger down his chest. That moment had been over way too soon.

Now, she delighted in the breadth of his chest, his subtle muscles, and the sprinkling of coarse, dark hairs over his skin.

His hot breath rushed across her cheek. "Let's go back to the bedroom."

Can we run?

He joined hands with her, then led her down the hall. In his room, she only had the vague impression of a soft-looking navy comforter on a pine bed before he yanked her against him and seized control of her mouth again.

He stripped off her jacket, and she let her head fall back, exposing her throat, offering her neck to his lips.

"Lily," James said as he pressed his mouth to her pulse.

The sensations he evoked sent ripples of pleasure down her spine. After all the scrambling and denying they'd both done, she could hardly believe she was finally here with him, her hunger finally being satiated.

He undressed her quickly, laid her on his bed, then shed his own clothes and joined her. She lay naked and exposed to him, and he took his time looking her over. She couldn't ever remember feeling so vulnerable to anyone. Sex had always been fun and light-hearted for her.

But tonight she was desperate to feel more, to have every touch and word mean more. To be perfect. Would she measure up?

When his gaze met hers, she sucked in a breath.

"You are the most beautiful woman I've ever seen."

Okay, that would be a *yes* for measuring up.

He grinned. "And I like the other tattoo."

She wrapped her hand around his neck and pulled him toward her breast. "I bet it tastes good, too."

The tasting led to heart-pounding need that couldn't be held back any longer. When their bodies joined, she arched her back and gripped his hips with her thighs, binding him to her, loving him with her body, since she was too afraid to say the words.

Throughout the night he explored her with his lips and his hands, and she returned the favor. They made love twice more before she dressed quietly in the predawn light, kissed his sleeping forehead, then crept back upstairs to her own apartment.

OVER THE NEXT WEEK, they spent every day and night together. During the day, they even sneaked off to his apartment to make love. She never would have expected James to be so adventurous—or unprofessional—but he seemed to throw himself whole-heartedly into their affair, smiling secretly when she'd walk into his office and telling her to close the door.

If Garnet noticed all the door closings and moony-eyed looks, she didn't say so. She was too busy doodling shoes all over everything. She spent hours looking through fabric and leather samples. She even asked about cost projections and profit margins.

Lily had told Fedora what was going on. She couldn't exactly disappear every night without the woman noticing. Of course, Fedora thought the idea of them together was terrific and probably thought Lily was just the thing to keep her son in the city.

Lily wasn't nearly so confident.

Though generally an optimistic person, she knew the bliss wouldn't last. James's retirement loomed over everything like a monster about to pounce. She knew one day she'd walk into the office and he'd tell her he was going to start interviewing candidates for his job. She pretended everything was perfect, though, while a very small part of her hoped he might change his mind and stay.

And what if he did? They'd move in together, they'd get...*married?*

People in love got married. At least where she was from. And though she'd spent a lot of years convincing herself that she was a hip, modern New Yorker, some of those Midwestern values just refused to die.

But she didn't want to settle down, did she? She wasn't ready for the responsibility of a commitment like marriage. Couldn't they just float along in the vague happy state of falling in love?

Of course, since she was the only one in love, it might be a short flight.

You should tell him. Tell him how you feel.

Oh, no. Because then the happiness would definitely end. James had plans, plans that certainly didn't include her. And she wasn't really sure what she'd do if he looked her in the eye now and told her so.

Wracked with indecision, she'd called Gwen. "Do you think I should bring up my feelings?"

"No."

"Do you think he'll bring it up?"

"No. The man is getting sex on a regular basis, Lily. Men have priorities."

Her conversation with Kristin had gone a similar way. "You've been sleeping together barely a week. Give it some time. Enjoy yourself."

But she was having a harder time by the hour. She was jumpy and unable to concentrate. If this was what love did to a woman, no wonder she'd gone out of her way to avoid it for so long.

The day before the Spectacular, as she sat at her drafting table and worked on a new set of sketches, he walked into the room and shut the door.

Her heart jumped. Was he going to kiss her, or give her the dreaded news?

She actually flinched when he slid his arm around her waist. *Oh, please, this is getting ridiculous.*

"Too much coffee?" he asked in her ear.

She turned her head, bringing their lips within inches. "A bit."

His eyes darkened in a way that had become as familiar as looking into a mirror at her own reflection. Her stomach rolled over. "I've missed you this morning."

"I just left your place an hour ago."

"An hour and twenty-three minutes ago."

Lily smiled. Who knew his obsessive time watching could be so charming? She moved a fraction closer. "Well then you'd better remind me what I have to look forward to later."

His lips met hers in a warm, easy, exploring kiss, and she sighed. Floating along in a vague happy state wasn't such a bad place to be, after all.

"Let's go out tonight," James said against her lips.

She leaned back. "Out?" The most they'd gone out in the last week was out of the bedroom to answer the door and accept the Chinese takeout.

"We'll go someplace nice. Celebrate the show."

"With Carlotta and Fabian and the others?"

"If you want."

She shook her head, looping her arms around his neck. "No way."

"We'll get dressed up."

She lifted her eyebrows. "I thought the wardrobe I've been sporting lately was popular."

Bracing his hands at her hips, he pulled her to the edge of the stool and wedged his body at the juncture of her thighs. "Then again it's cold and nasty outside. We could build a fire and stay in."

Like the night before last when they'd made love in front of the fire? Tempting… But maybe afterward. "Oh no, you don't. You're not backing out now. We're going to the Four Seasons."

"Your wish is my command, boss."

"In fact, I think I'll take the rest of the day off to primp and go shopping." She hopped off the stool and started toward the door.

James grabbed her hand and pulled her back against him. He stroked the side of her face. "I love to see you smile."

He loved her smile. How much longer before he fell for the rest of her?

She pressed her lips to his. "Hold down the fort for me." She danced away from him, floating and blissful.

During her day at Elizabeth Arden and trying on half the dresses in the fashion district, Lily concentrated on enjoying herself and putting the worries about her feelings, his feelings and the future out of her mind. It would all fall at her doorstep soon enough, anyway. She'd lived for the moment for years now. She wasn't about to change her thinking for a little thing like love.

Wardrobewise, she settled on green again—a low-cut gown that flowed down her body like her own skin, then flared out in a full skirt. The color had brought her luck the first night she'd gone to James's apartment, and she even found more shamrock tattoos. She figured he'd appreciate the attention to detail.

She also splurged on an elaborate Swarovski crystal choker and earrings. She pulled her hair up in a loose twist on top of her head, letting several tendrils fall around her face. The dress complemented her eyes, and she smoothed on perfumed lotion that made her skin glimmer.

But maybe it was the glow of happiness that made her shine from the inside out.

She walked out of her room and found Fedora sitting by the fire reading a book. "I hate to leave you here by yourself."

Fedora stared at her, openmouthed.

"What?" Lily looked behind her, then down at her dress. "What's wrong?"

Fedora sniffled. "You're so beautiful."

"Oh. Thanks." Lily walked across the room toward her. Seeing Fedora's gray eyes watery with tears always sent a jolt through her. Her and her son's eyes were so alike. And, come to think of it, she'd seen those tears a lot more the last few days. At first, she thought Fedora was just enjoying the idea of having her own space, being a "gal" in New York rather than an old married woman. But, apparently, there was a point in every woman's life when she needed someone else in her space, when being a partner with the one you loved was more important than asserting your independence.

A lesson Lily knew she should take to heart.

She sat on the arm of Fedora's chair. "Are you okay?"

"I used to get dressed up for Martin. He would take me to the Rainbow Room, and we'd look for movie stars." She yanked a tissue from the box on the table next to her and dabbed at her eyes. "That was a long time ago, of course."

The woman was miserable. And it was time to do something about it.

Fedora patted her hand. "Don't tell James I was crying. He'll worry." She rose from the chair. "I'm going to find my camera."

Love—true, abiding and deep. Fedora and Martin were the living, breathing embodiment of the emotion. Would she and James someday—

She cut herself off with a shake of her head. *You're living for the moment, enjoying yourself and him. That's it. It's all you have.*

While Fedora was in the guest room, Lily made a

phone call that would hopefully take care of at least somebody's relationship. And by the time James arrived ten minutes later, she had her emotions under control.

They posed for pictures, even though Lily thought it was a little too promlike, then Fedora waved them off.

"That reminded me just a little too much of my prom," James said in the elevator.

Lily glanced over at him. He looked breathtakingly handsome in a black suit and shirt, matched with a shiny, silver tie. Their thoughts running along the same path was happening more frequently. For two people who were supposedly so different, it was an odd sensation.

"As long as she doesn't have the picture blown up into an eleven-by-fourteen glossy and hang it over the fireplace, I'm fine with it."

He wrapped his finger around one of the curls brushing her shoulder. "Have I told you tonight how beautiful you look?"

She grinned. "Twice." She brushed her hand down his lapel. "But another time or two wouldn't necessarily be a bad thing."

"You look so perfect I'm almost afraid to touch you."

"Well, you'll have to get over that quick."

He laughed and slid his arm around her waist as they walked out of the elevator and through the lobby.

Outside, she stared at the long, black limo parked at the curb.

"Come on," he said, urging her toward the car. "It's fun."

As she passed through the open door, held by a uniformed driver, she recalled she'd said the same thing to him a couple of weeks ago. Oh, yeah, something odd was happening to them both. Were they really changing or just doing things that they knew made the other happy? And would any of it, ultimately, make a difference?

Dinner was elegant. James was charming. The food was delicious. Everything was perfect.

But Lily couldn't relax. Her stomach had twisted itself into a knot.

She couldn't do this anymore. She couldn't pretend she was happy with the way things were.

She was through with living for the moment. She wanted to know if James would be around tomorrow. She wanted to know if their relationship had him rethinking his retirement. She wanted to plan a future with him. And if that future included marriage, and even a house in the suburbs or a farm in Connecticut, she wanted to experience it. With him.

He was her partner in nearly every way already. He was her contrast, her balance. The reason her business had accomplished so much was because they'd worked *together.* Each giving their own talents and relying on their own strengths.

As long as she could continue to spend her days watching him smile at her, touching him, loving him, she was willing to do just about anything.

When they strolled outside, she tugged him away from the valet. "Let's walk a bit first."

"In those shoes?"

"We won't go far." They walked along Lexington Avenue, not looking at all out of place on the street, as you could find an eclectic mix most any time of the day or night.

Lily inhaled the crisp air. Was she really considering leaving the buzz and excitement of the city? Could she really do that—even for James?

She looked around at the lights and the people. Heard the sounds of horns and chatter, the click of heels on the sidewalk. For her, after the last few weeks of learning what it was like to share her life with the man she loved, it would be a pretty empty city without him in her life.

He slid his hands in his pants pockets, and she stared at the sidewalk. "You've been quiet tonight."

"Yeah. I guess so."

"Is everything all right?"

"I'm not sure." Oh, *that* made sense. She drew a deep breath. Time to jump in. "Are you still leaving?"

"Leaving where?"

She stopped and faced him. "Retiring. Leaving the city."

"Oh." He looked away, and she could see the answer on his face as plainly as if he'd said the words aloud.

He was going. She wasn't enough.

"I've already bought the farm," he said. "I've made plans—"

"I love you."

"You *what?*" He pulled her out of the path of walking traffic and in front of a deli. "What did you say?"

Lily met his gaze and pretended a half-dozen butterflies weren't batting around in her stomach. She'd taken the plunge. There was no point in backing out now. "I love you."

He shook his head, disbelief evident in his eyes. "Since when?"

"The day you came by the warehouse, and I was

painting the arch. You admitted you were looking up my dress, and you smiled at me."

"You know the exact *moment?*"

"It was a pretty special moment."

"It's not possible."

"It is. I do." He went pale, and she got angry. "What's wrong, James? Is this not part of your *plan?*"

He shoved his hand through his hair. "You're damn right it isn't. You're not the one I'm supposed to be with."

"Really?" She directed her pain into fury, or else she was afraid she'd break down and sob. "I'm not *normal* enough for you?"

"You're you. There's nothing wrong with that."

"Oh, I guess not. In fact, I was *perfect* when you wanted to get me into bed."

"That was—"

"And speaking of this last week—what was that about? Sex? A few laughs?"

"No, I—" He hung his head. "I have to go, Lily. I want something different than I have. I want to change my life."

"Without me."

"I'm going to Connecticut."

She grasped the lapels of his jacket and pulled him toward her. "I could go with you." Was she really pleading with him? What was wrong with her? He didn't want her. How many times did he have to tell her?

He shook his head. "You'd be miserable in a week."

"We've accomplished so much together. A little bit of you, a little bit of me. Why can't that work in a relationship?"

"Because we're too different. We'd argue all the time. Fights and drama. I've had enough." He paused and stared at the ground. "Being with you is…it's just too much."

Fights and drama? What the hell was he talking about? She'd had the most peaceful week of her life with him. And maybe it wouldn't always be that way, but then what relationship was ever—

The fights, the drama, the make-ups…

The words resonated inside her, sparking a memory. She remembered the night of Jose's performance, when they'd talked about his parents' relationship. "You're talking about your parents," she said slowly, releasing him. "You're scared. You think we'll end up like them."

"Yes."

"They're deeply in love. What's wrong with that?"

"They're also separated!" He lowered his voice as a group of people walking by looked their way. "They're volatile and unpredictable."

"You think you can plan out a relationship so that everything is always smooth and easy?"

"No, but I also know I don't want to be that much in love with anybody."

Lily stared at him as if she'd never seen him before. Her chest felt heavy, as if he'd just dropped a huge rock on her. Did anyone really have a choice? Why wouldn't he want to share something that powerful? She hadn't expected love, either, but she wasn't running from it.

Did he not want to fall in love with anybody? Or just her?

Again, it hardly mattered. She'd told him how she

felt. She'd been willing to give up the most precious thing she had—her life in New York. But she was through begging and reasoning.

She stepped back. "You want to go, then go. After the show tomorrow, I want you to leave. I'll find a new assistant on my own."

Looking cold and distant, James rolled his shoulders. "I don't feel comfortable abandoning you that way."

"That's just too damn bad. You're fired."

The tears finally rolled down her face as she turned around and walked away from him, melting into the crowd.

11

JAMES HAD TO DRAG HIMSELF out of bed the next morning. He usually thrived on the activity and challenges of show day. He usually looked forward to seeing the people in the audience point and gasp, then make plans to part with their hard-earned cash for the opportunity to have a pair of Lily's shoes. He usually enjoyed watching Lily's excitement.

Today he just wanted the whole awful business to be over with. He'd made his decision, and he was just ready to get on with his new life. He was relieved she'd told him to go. He couldn't imagine spending the next two months in the office with all that had passed between them.

At the exhibition hall, he avoided her. Like the coward he was, he turned the other direction when he saw her and went out of his way to make sure they didn't bump into each other.

And while he was being a selfish jerk, she got his parents back together.

It was just before the start of the show, and he was walking through the audience making sure the view of the stage was perfect from every angle. Then he saw Lily standing by the backstage curtain. His parents stood next to her, and he watched her join their hands, kiss them each on the cheek, then issue a fin-ger-wagging order.

His parents embraced each other, and he didn't have to be any closer to see the look in their eyes. His heart contracted.

But he turned away.

During the show, he looked at his watch a million times. He had to go. He couldn't wait to go. It was almost over.

I love you.

You're fired.

If he could just get away from her, he wouldn't hear those words anymore or see the contrasting looks in her eyes over and over, like a film reel stuck in a loop.

He slinked away while she was talking to a re-porter from *InStyle*. He raced to his apartment, packed a bag, then rented a car and sped out of the city, heading toward his farm and the peace he so desperately craved.

As he drove, James realized he should have known the harmony with Lily wouldn't last. He should have seen the scene from last night coming. A relationship with her could only end in disaster.

Wait. He *did* know. That's why he'd fought against their attraction in the first place.

He'd let her passion, her vitality and her body dis-tract him. She'd blown him off course. But only tem-porarily. The farther he got from the city, the more the pressure in his chest released.

He bought a dog—a silly chocolate Lab whose ears and feet were way too big for his body and who kept sliding across the wooden floors in the house.

He drove around town and searched for a vacant storefront to house his café. He bought groceries at the general store. He talked about cows and horses with a few guys at the hardware store.

He did all the things he was supposed to do, all the things he'd planned. With each small step into his new life, he'd forget about her.

Nearly two weeks after the Spectacular, James sat on his back porch swing and drank coffee, listening to the silence, while Cap—short for Cappuccino—gnawed on a bone at his feet. He needed the solace of this place. He didn't have to answer the phone, read contracts or sales projections. He didn't have to e-mail or fax anybody. He didn't have to solve a crisis.

His life and his time were his own. He could pick up his ambitions from fifteen years ago and make a new start.

Alone, if necessary.

And that was the biggest bunch of crap he'd ever tried to sell anyone.

He was the most *un*relaxed retired person on the planet. He was restless and bored and miserable. He missed the people. God, were there any *people* in this state? He was beginning to think cows outnumbered humans three to one.

He wanted a Reuben. He wanted to ride in a cab. He wanted to be pushed along by the crowds on Broadway.

He wanted Lily. He *had* to have her.

Without her laughter and energy he had nothing.

Oh, he needed solace and a retreat. And he did want to do something besides run somebody else's life. But he needed Lily way more.

He'd gladly take the drama and the chaos. He'd revel in the smiles and the tears. The fights and make-ups. He'd once feared loving her too much. He'd once thought a marriage like his parents wasn't for him.

What an idiot he'd been.

His parents' marriage was based on understanding, respect and love—true, one-and-only love. Why was he so afraid of that? Why had he pushed that away?

He didn't have a choice, anyway. He loved Lily with everything in him. Maybe he wasn't *supposed* to fall in love with her, but he had. His big plans meant nothing without her to share them.

She loves me.

He stared into the distance, barely seeing the pasture and barn. He marveled that she returned the feelings he now realized he'd felt for her from the very beginning. From the moment she'd laughed and tugged at her thigh-high stockings at their first show, he'd been a goner. He'd fought and tried to ignore his heart, but he'd pretty much fallen for her immediately. Maybe he'd been so stupid weeks ago because he couldn't believe she really felt that way about him. He certainly hadn't expected her declaration.

So that gave him the right to throw her feelings back at her?

He'd do anything to replay that night. But he didn't have that option. All he could do was move forward. To fix the disaster he'd created.

He refused to believe he'd fail. The solution was simple—to come up with a plan, a new plan, that she absolutely couldn't resist.

"GARNET, THE ORDERS for the new leather pumps aren't here," Lily called from the floor of her workroom.

She heard Garnet stalk down the hall. "And you call me a bad filer," she said when she appeared in the doorway.

Lily glanced at the piles of papers spread around her, each one held in place by a different shoe. "I know where everything is." Frowning, she paused. "*Except* for the leather-pump orders."

"I could look in Ja—" She stopped and flushed. "In *his* office."

Lily rolled her eyes. "You can say his name, you know. I'm not going to fall apart."

"You did yesterday."

"Just go look."

Garnet flounced off, and Lily went through the pile under the yellow sandal again. Maybe she'd missed the order the first time.

"Garnet, did you find it yet?" she called several minutes later when the receptionist—correction, her new protégée—still hadn't appeared.

Thanks to Gwen, they'd been busy interviewing candidates for a new office manager and receptionist, especially critical now, with two designers in the company. With the Spectacular a roaring success and the spring collection selling like crazy, she'd started on design ideas for the fall and found her confidence had grown, her understanding of her business had deepened.

Officewise, she and Garnet had survived the last two weeks—not happily, and certainly not smoothly, but they'd pressed on. She was going to make it without him—not happily, and probably not smoothly at first—but she was determined not to wallow. This was her business. She'd built it. She loved it. She'd never give it up. Not for anyone.

"Hi."

Lily glanced up with a jolt. James was leaning against the door frame, a panting, chocolate-colored puppy on a leash beside him.

Blinking, she wondered if she was imagining him. But, oh, boy, she wasn't sure she could conjure him up in her mind as clearly, looking quite so good. So perfect. He wore tailored black slacks and a gray sweater that matched his eyes.

And the dog was pretty cute, too.

Stay steady, girl. You knew this moment was going to come.

She swallowed. "Here to clear out your stuff?"

"No."

She wanted to get up. She probably looked like an idiot sitting barefoot in the middle of the floor with an entire file cabinet of paper scattered around her. Definitely not professional or organized.

She lifted her chin. She was adapting as best she could, but she wasn't going to pretend to be someone she wasn't, either. "Why are you here, then?"

He walked toward her, the dog's feet sliding clumsily on the wooden floor. They made quite a picture. An *adorable* picture.

Women can't resist a man and a cute puppy, right?

Her heart squeezed in pain. Had they really once laughed and teased each other? Been close and shared their dreams? She couldn't think past the moment he'd pushed her away, rejecting her offer of love.

He kept moving until he was only a foot away,

then he knelt beside her. The scent of his cologne drifted toward her, and memories she'd spent two weeks locking away came rushing back. The night they'd made love in front of the fire. The exasperated smile on his face the day she'd surprised him with the manicure and pedicure. The proud smile on his lips as he'd helped her into the limo on the way to the Four Seasons. The day in the warehouse when she'd realized she loved him.

The dog licked her hand, bringing her out of the past.

She shifted her attention to him and rubbed the top of his soft head.

"Cap, this is Lily. Lily, Cap."

Lily scratched the dog under the chin, and he blissfully leaned into her and closed his eyes. "Cap? He looks more like a Chocolate or Cocoa."

"He prefers Cappuccino."

She looked up, meeting James's gaze. "Oh." She did too. He used to bring her cappuccino from Starbucks when he first came to work for her. Then, at Christmas, he'd bought her a machine of her own. "Are you ever going to tell me why you're here?" she asked coolly.

"Yeah. I'm just nervous, I guess. I need to ask a favor."

"A favor?" He *had* to be kidding. She glared at him, and he had the grace to flush.

He cleared his throat. "You see…" James paused, and his eyes shone with emotion, an emotion so pure and strong, she found herself holding her breath. "I subleased my apartment and put the farm in Connecticut on the market, so Cap and I are homeless at the moment. We were wondering if we could stay here a while."

She didn't dare move. "You put the farm on the market? Why?"

He let go of Cap's leash and brushed his thumb across her cheek. "Because the woman I love is here."

"But you...you said—"

He laid his finger over her lips. "I was an idiot, and I said a lot of idiotic things. Starting with you not being part of my stupid plan and ending somewhere around being too scared to admit my feelings. What I *didn't* say was the most important thing—I love you." His voice lowered almost to a whisper. "I love you more than anything."

Her pulse thrummed and sweat pooled at the base of her spine. She wanted to believe in this turnaround, but the memory of his rejection was fresh and raw. "You spent two weeks on a farm and got bored, so now you're back?"

"No. Well, yeah, I was bored, but that's not why I'm back. I'm back because I had to see you, to apologize, to try to change the way I screwed up everything that night."

"Because you realized you love me." Lily snapped her fingers. "Just like that."

He smiled. "It was just like that, but not at that—" He held up his finger. "Let me get something that will help." He rose and walked out of the room, the dog bounding after him.

Desperate to focus on something besides the emotions shooting through her veins, Lily shook her head. Good grief, when that dog grew into his feet he was going to weigh eighty pounds, at least. What was James going to do with a dog that size in Manhattan?

James returned with two big, rectangular, brown-wrapped packages, which he laid side by side on the drafting table. He held out his hand toward her. "Come see."

On shaky legs, Lily rose and laid her hand in his. He drew her to the table. She'd so deeply wanted him to come back, to apologize and say all the things he was saying, that she wanted to pinch herself to make sure she wasn't dreaming. She hadn't dared voice her wish or hope too hard that it would come true. Yet, here he was.

"These are the two most important moments in my life," he said.

She glanced sideways at him. Moments in plain brown wrappers?

"Open them. The one on the left first."

She tore the wrapper down the center, revealing a photograph in a professionally matted, gold frame. The picture was a blowup of the one in his apartment, taken on the night of their first show together.

"Remember the night you saw this, and you were surprised I could recall all those details about what you were wearing and what you did and said?"

Tears springing to her eyes, Lily nodded, running her finger along the edge of the frame.

"I could do that because that was the moment I fell in love with you." He laid his finger beneath her chin and turned her face toward his. "A moment like that is pretty special, so it stood out."

Her breath hitched in her throat, and she threw her

arms around him. She buried her face against his neck and simply breathed in his love.

Then she pressed her lips to his, pouring all the frustration and fear of the last two miserable weeks into a healing touch. She'd never let him go again. She'd fight for them, for the love they shared.

They finally broke apart, though he still held her tight against his chest. "You haven't even seen the other one."

She dabbed at her eyes with the pads of her fingers. "I don't know if I can take another one."

James brushed her hair away from her face. "Try."

Keeping one arm around him, she used her other hand to tear open the second package. It was another picture in a matching frame. This one was of them the night they'd dressed up and gone to the Four Seasons.

"The night you said you loved me," he said softly against her cheek.

She remembered the fear and uncertainty of that night, then the pain that came later, but after today, she thought she'd look at their smiling faces with an affection and appreciation for the day their lives together had really begun.

"Can you say it again?" he asked, his voice breaking. "Please tell me I didn't destroy it."

She framed his face with her hands. "I love you. I love your smile and your patience. I love that you support me and challenge me. I love your professionalism." She glanced over at the messy piles of files and paper on the floor. "I especially love your ability to file."

"I don't think I have to help with that. You fired me, you know."

"You were breaking my heart at the time."

"How about I spend the next sixty years mending it?"

Lily grinned. "That's a plan."

EPILOGUE

"IT WAS A LOVELY wedding," Lily said as she stretched out on the sofa.

James lay on his side next to her, burying his face in her hair and nuzzling her neck, and she reveled in the familiar planes of his body, which could still make her tremble every single time he touched her. "A bit unconventional."

"But perfect for your parents."

"Ours will be better."

She raised her eyebrows. "We're actually going through with it?"

"You have to. It's costing a fortune."

"You don't think it will make us a boring, old suburban couple?"

"God, I hope so. You and Garnet are making everybody crazy with this new show."

She swatted him on the chest. "You're just jealous you're not in the middle of the action anymore."

She'd hired a new office manager six months ago so that James could go to cooking school. She'd put on nearly ten pounds as a result, but each and every ounce had been delicious, and his joy at doing something besides organize had compounded her satisfaction.

They'd also been busy leasing the apartment next

to Lily's, then knocking down walls to make a bigger space, complete with an extralarge kitchen. They'd fought over whose bed they'd use every night, but the making up—and ultimately deciding every bed in the apartment should get equal time— had been a memory Lily would always cherish.

Garnet had transitioned into her new role as an up-and-coming shoe designer with dedication and enthusiasm. And Lily had acquired a new assistant— nerdy Ricky Desmond, the computer geek who came with a built-in crush on Gwen but still organized like a maniac. They'd hired a new receptionist, as well. Unfortunately, she was one of Garnet's friends, so nobody still got their correct messages.

She'd also convinced James not to sell the farm in Connecticut, after all, and they spent most weekends up there with their dogs—Cap and his very pregnant mate, Latte—and even a few cows. It was a great place to slow down and take time to be together without all the distractions and rush of the city.

He rubbed his thumb across her bottom lip. "You're going to make a beautiful bride. Have I told you today how lucky I am to have you?"

"I think you did this morning, but I could stand to hear it again."

His eyes darkened, his devotion to her obvious. "I love you, and I'm so grateful you love me."

Just before Lily kissed him, she glanced at the pair of gold-framed portraits above the fireplace, remembering the day their new lives had begun. Her happiness spread down to the tips of her toes.

Currently boasting a pair of lime-green stiletto sandals.

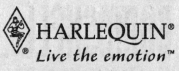

If you enjoyed what you just read,
then we've got an offer you can't resist!

Take 2 bestselling
love stories FREE!
Plus get a FREE surprise gift!

Harlequin Romance®

Contract Brides

From paper marriage...to wedded bliss?

A *wedding dilemma:*

What should a sexy, successful bachelor do if he's too busy
making millions to find a wife? Or if he finds the perfect
woman, and just has to strike a bridal bargain...?

The *perfect proposal:*

The solution? For better, for worse, these grooms in a hurry
have decided to sign, seal and deliver the ultimate
marriage contract...to buy a bride!

Coming Soon to

HARLEQUIN®
Romance®

featuring the favorite miniseries Contract Brides:

THE LAST-MINUTE MARRIAGE
by Marion Lennox, #3832
on sale February 2005

A WIFE ON PAPER
by award-winning author Liz Fielding, #3837
on sale March 2005

VACANCY: WIFE OF CONVENIENCE
by Jessica Steele, #3839
on sale April 2005

Available wherever Harlequin books are sold.

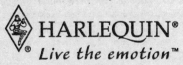

The world's bestselling romance series.

Seduction and Passion Guaranteed!

Mamma Mia!

They're tall, dark...and ready to marry!

Don't delay. Order the next story in
this great new miniseries...pronto!

On sale in January
THE ITALIAN'S TOKEN WIFE
by *Julia James* #2440

Furious at his father's ultimatum, Italian millionaire
Rafaello di Viscenti vows to marry the first woman he sees—
Magda, a single mother desperately trying to make ends meet
by doing his cleaning! Rafaello's proposal comes with a
financial reward, so Magda has no choice but to accept....

**Pick up a Harlequin Presents® novel and you will enter a world
of spine-tingling passion and provocative, tantalizing romance!**

Available wherever Harlequin Books are sold.

www.eHarlequin.com HPTITW0105